THE TIDE ALSO RISES
BY
MAC FORTNER

Books by Mac Fortner

<u>THE CAM DERRINGER SERIES:</u>

KNEE DEEP

BLOODSHOT

KEY WEST: TWO BIRDS, ONE STONE

MURDER FEST KEY WEST

HEMINGWAY'S TREASURE

SAME OLD SONG

THE BAHAMA BLUES

THE WRONG KEY

LOOSE LIPS SINK SHIPS

WATER, WATER EVERYWHERE

DEEP BLUE ALIBI

DEEP BLUE DECEPTION

CHASING THE TIDE

THE TIDE ALSO RISES

<u>THE SUNNY RAY SERIES: TRILOGY</u>

RUM CITY BAR

THE BATTLE FOR RUMORA

THE SOVEREIGN SISTER

<u>CAM'S WOMEN SERIES</u>

KAILEY

Sign up for my NEWSLETTER[1] and receive the latest on my releases and other Tropical News.

www.macofortner.com

Published by: Tan Toes Publishing

Edited by: Caroline Vaught

Cover Design by: Mac Fortner

Dedication

I'm dedicating this book to the memory of **Jimmy Buffett**, a man who transcended far beyond our expectations. Through his music and lifestyle, he allowed millions of us to live out our dream lives. We sang along at concerts, donning our wildest shark hats and parrot-head gear. We knew the words to every song and didn't care that we didn't sound good singing them. Who else could make us act that way?

We may have lost him as a physical being, but his spirit will always remain. So (FINS UP) and remember to keep living life on your own terms. Goodbye Jimmy: you will grace heaven with your voice.

Prologue

I was sitting on the rear deck of my boat reading a brochure about a small village on the Yucatan Peninsula. Its name is Playa El Cuyo. It's a pictural village surrounded by palm trees.

I googled it and looked at the hundreds of pictures. It looked like what I'd been searching for. It wasn't crowded with tourists; most of the people spoke English, and it was far away from here.

I picked up my guitar and played a few Jimmy Buffett songs while I thought about his recent death. I'll miss that man. He was more than a musician; he was a lifestyle.

I played a few songs of my own. They were tropical songs as well. Maybe not in the same class as Jimmy's, but I think they're good.

I'll take a margarita on the rocks
A little lime and a little salt
If I get crazy, it ain't my fault
Just blame it on the lime, blame it on the salt

I decided to not quit my day job.

I felt something on my foot and looked down. Walter was sitting on it. I believe he wanted some attention.

"Wanna go for a run?" I asked him in his doggy language.

He just stared at me. Usually, he goes wild and grabs his leash off the wall. Instead, he licked my leg.

"We'll stop at Betty's." It was his favorite donut shop, and mine.

He jumped up, ran to the door, grabbed his leash off the wall, and went to the gate, where he stood and wiggled all over. He probably needed his sugar fix.

"Okay, give me a minute."

I went inside and put on my running shoes, grabbed a bottle of water, and returned to the deck. Walter was gone.

"Walter!" I called as I followed the dock toward the parking lot.

When I walked past Stacy's boat, she was sitting on the back deck laughing.

"What's funny?" I asked.

"Walter," she said.

"What did he do now?"

"He ran past here with his leash in his mouth, squeezed through the gate, and took off for the road."

"Crap."

"Where did you tell him you were going?"

"Betty's."

"He'll see ya there. Bring me a chocolate honeybun."

I waved goodbye to Stacy and ran up the dock. Walter's the weirdest dog I've ever seen. He doesn't even have any money with him.

• • • •

THE TWELVE-FOOT TENDER slipped into the docks at the El Cuyo Marina. It was greeted by two young boys eager for a tip for tying off the skiff and fueling it when necessary for the men on board. They've been waiting for this boat every day now for three weeks.

The men return at the same time every day. The boys have seen their big boat anchored in the bay. Every day, it goes out with them, and then it comes back, and the men come to shore here in the skiff.

"Hello, boys," Lucas Gardner said as he stepped off the boat. "Fill 'er up."

The boys scrambled to be the first one to get the nozzle and fill the tank.

"Mister Luke, did you find a treasure today?"

"No, nothing today, but one day we will."

"I hope so."

"When we do, I'll make you both rich."

"Hey, boys," Casey Rhodes said as he handed out a duffel bag.

The boy who lost at the fueling job grabbed the bag and hoisted it to the dock. Casey stepped off the boat and retrieved the bag.

"Is it full of treasures?" the boy asked.

"You better believe it," Casey said. "Look."

He pulled the bag open, and the boy eagerly looked inside. He pulled his head back and wrinkled his nose. "Those are just rocks," he said.

"Yeah, but they're pretty rocks. You can take them to town to *Treasures From The Deep* and sell them. I'll split it with ya."

The store sat on the beach about a half-mile away. It sold anything it could make people think came from the ocean. Casey always found something for them. It didn't pay him much, but it was fun.

"Okay, Mister Casey," the boy said and hefted the bag over his shoulder. He took off down the dock, staggering under the weight.

The two men started walking toward the Naia Café.

"I'm starving," Casey said. "Diving 'll wear ya out."

"We need to stock up on food so we don't have to come in here every night."

They were halfway there when a Jeep pulled up beside them. "Hey, you guys need a ride?" the passenger asked in a strong Mexican accent.

"Yeah, thanks," Casey said as they hopped into the back seat.

"Where ya goin'?"

"Naia."

"Oh, good food. My cousin owns that place," one of them said.

"Naia?"

"Yeah, she's an excellent cook."

"The best," Luke said.

They drove a few blocks and turned right down an alley.

"Where you goin'?" Luke asked, knowing this was not the way to Naia's.

"Shortcut."

"Bullshit," Casey said and stood in the back seat, ready to jump out.

The passenger turned in his seat and pointed a pistol at the two men. "Sit!"

Casey sat back down. "We only have enough money with us to get something to eat," he said.

"We don't want your money, señor."

The driver kept moving down the alley until he came out on another street. He turned left and drove to the next corner, where he turned right and pulled over to the side of the road in front of Naia's.

"Here ya go. I told you it was a shortcut."

"Sorry about that," Casey said.

"I wanted to show you how easy it would be to kidnap you and kill you. No one would ever know."

"Why would you want to show us that?" Luke asked.

"Because we want half of everything you raise from our sea."

"Half of everything? You're crazy. I ain't givin' you jack shit."

"You will, Mister Luke, or I will take it all and your boat."

Casey and Luke stared at each other, weighing their options. Rumors of a gang haunting the area had been circulating for weeks. If they didn't pay them off, their lives were in danger.

The two men got out of the car and watched the Jeep drive away. They knew that Pedro's crew had been behind the extortion attempt.

Their hearts pounded in their chests as they heard the roar of the Jeep driving away, echoing in the alleyways. They could hear their shallow breaths as they contemplated what to do next.

The smoky aroma of burned rubber and synthetic gasoline from the Jeep lingered in the air. A hint of fear fell upon the two men.

Rumors swirled that Pedro and his gang were wreaking havoc in the small town. They'd been squeezing money out of unsuspecting businesses for years, from dockside bars to fishing fleets—no one was safe. If you tried to resist well, you wouldn't want to find out what happened next. Wealth through intimidation seemed like a lucrative way of life for Pedro and his crew.

"Let's get some groceries and get out of here," Casey said. "We'll stay on the boat from now on. When we need supplies, we'll get them from Holbox."

"The sooner, the better," Luke said.

They went to the store and picked up what little they had available. They thought it would be enough to last a week.

When they returned to the dock, they were surprised to that their boat was gone. One of the boys was standing on the dock.

"Mario, where's my boat?" Luke asked him.

"The men took it. I tried to stop them, but they hit me. They said to tell you they would be back in one hour to get you."

"What men?"

"Bad men."

Chapter 1

When I arrived at Betty's bakery, Walter was waiting for me. "What the hell, boy? Can't you even wait for me so you won't get hit by a car?"

Betty opened the door. "I wondered if you were with him. He wouldn't come in until you arrived."

"Yeah, he doesn't have any money."

"He has credit here. He stopped by last week and got three donut holes."

I looked at Walter. He looked away.

"Well, at least I got my run in," I said, slightly out of breath.

"You know, you're a lot more fun since you got that dog," she said.

"Yeah, he's a good running partner. He has more energy than me!"

"He has four legs. You only have two."

"Good point. We'll stop back for our rolls after the run."

"I'll save a few donut holes and a chocolate honey bun. Make that two. Stacy wants one."

We laughed and said our goodbyes. Walter and I started walking down the street.

"Let's go for a run to the beach," I suggested. "It will be nice to get some fresh air and stretch our legs."

He didn't say anything, so I figured he was up for it.

Finally, after what felt like an eternity of running, we reached our destination––Higgs Beach! A swath of white sand stretched out before us as far as our eyes could see while crystal-clear waves lapped at its edges. Seagulls flew overhead squawking happily as they rode on thermals created by the heat of the day. We stopped to take it all in before continuing on our way along the shoreline until we reached the pier jutting out from the sand, where we decided to rest for a moment to admire our surroundings further still––taking in every detail from faraway sailboats gliding across distant waters to tiny crabs scurrying around near our feet.

"This is the life, Walter."

He sat down and stared at the water. I don't know what he was thinking, but he looked to be deep in thought. He could look so wise sometimes and other times...

A few minutes later, we walked up the beach to Salute—a restaurant on Higgs Beach. I bought two hot dogs, put mustard on one, and gave the other to Walter, who devoured it before I could take a bite. Then he looked at mine.

"No way, Jose. I've told you a million times to eat slowly."

He pretended not to understand English. It's his favorite trick.

Finally, when he realized I wasn't going to give him any of mine, he started to sniff the ground in hopes a part of his had fallen down there. He found a little piece of bun and licked it into his mouth.

When I finished, I let him lick the wrapper. He seemed satisfied.

"You ready to head back to Betty's?"

As soon as he heard the name, he jumped up and started running in place. I held the leash tightly.

The run to Betty's was easy because he pulled me most of the way there. We got our rolls and headed back to the boat. Along the way, I told Walter about the adventure he was about to embark on.

"We're going to the Yucatan Peninsula," I told him. "It's a small town called El Cuyo. It won't be crowded so you can run on the beach all day. I also heard they have a great donut shop there."

He looked up at me when I said, "Donut."

• • • •

LUKE AND CASEY WAITED at the docks for their tender to return. Even though they knew it wasn't going to be good, there was nowhere else to go. They couldn't just go off and leave their salvage boat three hundred yards off the coast. Casey had a lot of money tied up in that boat.

"I say," Casey said, "when we get back on the boat, we wait until dark and get the hell out of here. We haven't seen any sign of *The Tide*. She might not even be around here."

"She's here. I know the maps are right. It's just been so long that she has shifted and is probably mostly buried. She was one of the first ironclad ships put into service. I think there's a chance she might still be intact. We just have to find and uncover her."

"It's been two hundred and forty years since it sank. It could be completely covered."

"I didn't want to jinx us, but those pretty rocks you have been finding..."

"Yeah."

"They don't belong here. They came from the ship's ballasts. The ship was carrying two tons of gold and silver coins. They would still need a little weight before they picked the gold up. Some stones they would keep aboard to counterbalance the ship.

"The Spanish brig-of-war, *The Tide,* struggled against a storm until the battle was lost, and the ship and its treasure sank in the Gulf of Mexico, right here."

Casey did a quick calculation in his head. "Depending on how much was gold and how much was silver, it could be worth over a hundred million dollars."

"That's right."

"We can't let them take our find after we've spent all this time searching for it," Casey said.

"Let's tell them we can't find anything. That we were getting ready to leave the area," Luke said.

"Or we can move our boat about a mile to the east. There was a Dutch warship that sunk there in the eighteenth century. The Yucatan governor at the time blamed it on the north winds. I saw it when we were mapping *The Tide*."

"How's that going to help?"

"We use our DPVs. We can cover the distance quickly. They'll think we're diving the Dutch ship."

Luke scratched his head and thought it over a bit. He knew that Casey was right. They have two dive propulsion vehicles on board. They hadn't used them for a long time, and could need some maintenance before they could be put in the water. "What would we be lookin' for on the Dutch ship? They'll think we're crazy."

Casey shrugged. "I don't know. Artifacts, I guess. We'll have to bring one up every once in a while."

"Yeah, if we can find the ship."

Then they heard the sound of a boat motor. They looked toward the entrance to the marina. "There's our tender," Casey said.

"Yeah, its got two men in it."

The boat pulled to where they were standing and bumped the dock.

"Hey, amigos let's go," a heavy local man said, smiling and pointing a gun at them.

Casey and Luke picked up their supplies and sat them in the boat.

They idled out of the marina and turned toward their seventy-eight-foot custom salvage boat, *Malinda's Star*.

Chapter 2

When they arrived at the dive boat, they saw another man on board. He had a gun. The man introduced himself as Carlos. He said he would stay there with them while they dive to get the treasures.

Casey and Luke exchanged glances as they climbed aboard. "What's going on?" Casey asked cautiously.

Carlos stepped forward, his gun still pointed at them. "I am here to make sure you don't try anything funny when you are searching for the treasure," he said gruffly.

Casey and Luke looked at each other again, both of them thinking the same thing: how did this guy know about their plan?

Carlos didn't give them time to think about it too long, though. He and the other two quickly set up a perimeter around the boat and told them that they would be diving for three hours and then returning to shore with whatever treasures they could find.

"But we've been looking for the boat for weeks now. I don't think it's down there," Luke said.

"It's down there," Carlos said, his eyes drilling into Luke's. "Find it or you're a dead man."

One of the other men said, "About a half-mile in that direction." He pointed to the north-east.

"Are you sure?" Casey asked.

"I've seen it."

Luke pulled the anchor as Casey started the boat. They moved to the spot where the man told them to stop and dropped anchor again.

Casey and Luke got prepared for their dive, putting on their wetsuits and gathering all of their equipment before heading down into the depths of the Gulf of Mexico in search of *The Tide* and its lost treasure.

As soon as they got into the water, Casey took out his metal detector and started sweeping it in a wide arc around him.

As they descended deeper into the depths of the sea, Casey felt an eerie presence surrounding him as if something menacing was watching him from below; however, despite this feeling of dread, the two adventurers remained focused on their mission.

Casey pulled his board and marker from his waist belt and started to write. He held it up for Luke to see. *We've got to get them out of here.*

Luke took the board and wiped it clean, then wrote, *In time. Be careful.*

He wiped it clean again and gave it back to Casey, who hung it back on his belt.

They searched a new area for twenty minutes before Casey heard the metal detector beep. First slowly, then faster. He moved closer to the sandy floor and brushed away the sand. Something hard slightly emerged from the murky cloud of dust. They both started moving the sand, exposing more of the object. Finally, they could see the outline of a chest. It was about a foot deep and two feet long.

Together, they wrestled it out of its hold and set it on the ocean floor where they could get a good look. It had a rusted lock on it.

They looked at each other and gave high fives. In their excitement, they forgot about the trouble overhead. When they calmed down again, Casey pulled the board out and wrote, *We have to hide it.*

Luke nodded his head. They spotted a large bolder where they could tuck the chest into one of its caverns. Together they half-carried and half-scooted the chest into place. They covered it with sand again, and Casey gave Luke a thumbs up.

They turned and continued their search.

• • • •

I STOPPED AT STACY'S boat and handed her the sack. "Here ya go."

"Did Walter get his donut?" she asked.

"He had a hand full of donut holes. He's good for another week."

"What have you been reading over there all morning?"

"A brochure on El Cuyo. Walter and I are going to take a little trip."

"Oh, I wanna go," she said excitedly.

"Sorry, men only."

Stacy pouted. "You're no fun."

"Yes, I am. I'm going to El Cuyo."

I turned and walked to my boat.

I decided I had better call Diane and let her know I was going to be gone for a week.

"I wanna go too," she said.

"Not this time. It's just the guys."

"That's a stupid rule."

"Don't you have a business to run?"

"Yeah, but I can get away next week."

"I'm going this week."

"When will you leave?"

"Tomorrow morning," I said, suddenly making up my mind.

"What are ya doing tonight?"

"Well, Kailey is out of town, somewhere, so I guess I'm having supper with you if you want to."

"I have a date with Jack. Can I bring him?"

"Of course. I'll get some steaks and ask Stacy."

"Sounds good. I'm hungry."

"See ya about six."

I walked back to Stacy's boat. She was on the rear deck with Hank, eating her chocolate honeybun. There was a tall glass of milk sitting on the table.

"How do you get Hank to just sit there without trying to steal your roll?" I asked, thinking about Walter. He's a donut hound.

"I put hot sauce on the first bite I ever gave him. Now he doesn't want any more."

"Smart. It's probably too late to do that with Walt."

"What's up? Did you come back to invite me to El Cuyo? I'll wear my new bikini."

"As tempting as that is, I just came to invite you to supper with Diane and Jack."

She looked as though she was thinking it over. "Well, I guess that's better than nothing."

"Gee, thanks. I hope I'm not putting you out."

"I'll move a few things around."

"Okay," I said and turned to leave.

"Cam!"

I turned back toward her. She grabbed my face and kissed me on the lips. She tasted like chocolate.

"I love you," she said.

"You're still not going to El Cuyo."

I spent the rest of the day preparing the boat for the voyage. I went to the store and got steaks for the night and then all the supplies I thought I would need for the trip.

Stacy, who had been quiet for most of the meal, suddenly spoke up. "Hey, Cam, do you think we could try treasure diving around El Cuyo? It could be a fun little adventure."

I looked at her skeptically. "Are you serious? You know how dangerous that could be?"

"But think about it, Cam. We could be rich beyond our wildest dreams."

I shook my head. "Sorry, Stacy. Count me out. I'm not risking my life for some mythical treasure."

I asked Jack if he could get away and go with me to El Cuyo.

"I wish I could, but I have charters lined up all week."

"I'll go," Stacy said.

"Next time."

We finished our meal while talking about the possibility of finding a treasure, and as I cleaned up the dishes, I couldn't shake the feeling that something was off. It was as if the ocean was calling out to me, beckoning me to come explore its depths. But I knew better than to listen to that siren song. The ocean was full of dangers, and I didn't want to end up as some of those treasure hunters do.

As we said our goodbyes, I promised them I would take them another time. But now, I had a trip to El Cuyo to plan, and I was looking forward to some much-needed relaxation. But little did I know that fate had other plans for me.

Chapter 3

Casey and Luke searched for another half-hour before they were stopped in their tracks. Ahead of them, looming large, was the outline of a ship. They looked at each other wide-eyed, then swam toward it. This was it, *The Tide*.

They swam around the ship, exploring the cavities. It was mostly intact. That was amazing after two centuries under water. There were plenty of barnacles and schools of fish had made it their home. It had become a place of shelter for those who needed a fast place to escape to. It was beautiful.

Luke pointed at his tank and then the surface. Casey nodded and pulled a marker balloon from his pouch. He tied the line to *The Tide* and filled the balloon with his air. The balloon drifted to the surface when he released it.

They surfaced, feeling excited. The first thing they saw was a rifle pointing at them.

"Where's the treasure?" Carlos asked.

"We still didn't find anything. I don't think it's here," Casey said.

"Everyone knows it's here," Carlos said. "Either bring us something, or we'll have to kill you."

"I tell you, there's nothing down there."

"Get up here!"

They climbed onto the dive platform and removed their tanks. When they stood, Carlos swung the butt of his gun and hit Luke in the head, knocking him to the deck.

"Hey!" Casey yelled, "There's no reason for that. We've been looking for weeks and have found nothing."

"Look again!" he yelled.

Carlos glanced down at their gear. "What's that?" he asked, pointing to the board. "Hide what?"

Casey looked at the board. He had forgotten to erase the last message.

"It's nothing. I was just talking to my friend."

Carlos grabbed the board and read the message. "You didn't want me to read this? What are you hiding?"

Casey looked at Luke, who was still lying on the deck. He had to think fast. "We found something down there, but we were worried that if we brought it up, you would take it. We were trying to hide it."

Carlos looked suspicious. "What did you find?"

"We found a map. It looks like an old pirate map. We don't know what it leads to."

Carlos smiled. "Let's go take a look at this map."

Casey and Luke looked at each other in relief. They had bought themselves some time.

"I have to refill my tanks," Casey said. "Let me do that and we'll go down."

"Hurry."

Casey took his and Luke's tanks to the refill station. He bled a little air and checked the pressure. Eight hundred, that was good. He connected the valve and filled the tank, then did the same for Luke's. He went to the cabin door and opened it.

"Where are you going?" Carlos asked.

"Bathroom," Casey answered.

"Don't take long."

Casey went to the cabin and found an old map rolled in a waterproof tube they had purchased from a young boy in the Bahamas two years ago, and a small pry bar. They had checked the map out a year ago and found it was duplicated from an earlier find. The treasure was already gone. He stuffed them in his wet suit and returned to the deck.

"Are you ready?" Casey asked after checking his tank

"You go. I will be here with your friend. If you don't bring the map back, I will kill him."

Casey and Luke exchanged looks. Casey nodded. Luke's shoulders dropped in relief.

"I'll be back in a few minutes," Casey said.

He went to the platform, put his tank on, and dropped into the water.

Casey swam to the chest and pulled the small crowbar out of his suit. He put it in the lock and forced it until it broke open. He removed the lock and opened the chest.

Air escaped his mask as he gasped at the treasure that lay inside the trunk. He grabbed his mask, clearing it, and replaced it over his face.

He fell back, sitting on the ocean floor. Shining at him was a chest full of gold trinkets and precious stones. Necklaces and bracelets glittered in the turquoise water. He had found the treasure they had been seeking after months of planning.

There was no way he was going to let these pirates steal his treasure. He closed the chest and left the crowbar laying beside it. He pulled the map from his waistband and held the antique tube it was rolled in.

He swam to the surface again and climbed the platform.

"Do you have the map?" Carlos asked.

"Here," Casey said, handing it to him. "Just take it and let us be."

Carlos opened the tube and pulled out the map. He unrolled it and studied it carefully.

"Do you know where this is?"

"I haven't looked at the map yet. Let me see it."

He handed the map back to Casey. He opened it and pretended to be studying it.

"Yeah, I can find the area, but still, we would have to find the treasure on the bottom somewhere."

Carlos looked around and saw that the other two had left.

"Let's go," he said. "I will split the treasure with you."

"What about your boss?"

"Screw him. I want the treasure for myself."

"Let's do it then," Casey said. "I'll fire the boat up, and we'll get underway."

Without another word, Casey lunged at Carlos. He grabbed Carlos' arm and used his momentum to throw him back against the railing. Carlos stumbled, and before he could recover, Casey had knocked him out with one punch.

Casey grabbed the drag line and dove back into the water to retrieve the treasure chest.

When he surfaced, he said, "Help me pull this up."

Luke looked at Casey, then at the men standing on the deck. Casey had not seen them.

"Very good," the man said. "Help him."

Casey's shoulders slumped. Together they pulled the line until the chest broke the surface.

The men picked the chest up and carried it to the table on the rear deck. They opened it, exposing the jewels and gold.

"Thank you," he said to Casey. "I am Saulo. Pedro sent me to get you. You can go home now."

"He said you would split that with us," Luke said.

"That was before you killed Carlos."

"Carlos isn't dead," Casey said.

Saulo pulled his gun from his belt, pointed it at Carlos, and pulled the trigger.

"Yes, he is," Saulo said and laughed.

· · · ·

THE SUN PEEKED OVER the horizon, its golden light filtering through the curtains of my stateroom. Walter yawned beside me, his tail thumping against the mattress. Time to get up.

I swung my legs off the edge of the bed and stood, stretching my arms above my head. My shoulders popped as I felt the muscles stretch through my torso.

After splashing cold water on my face, I made my way up to the helm of my Kadey Korgen 55. The sea was calm this morning, gentle waves lapping at the hull of my boat. Perfect weather for the crossing to El Cuyo.

"Ready for an adventure, Walter?" I scratched the fur behind his ears. He barked in response, his tail wagging eagerly.

After taking him to do his business, we motored out of the marina as the sun climbed higher in the sky, its golden light transforming into a bright, tropical glare. I slipped on my sunglasses and set the autopilot, leaning back in the captain's chair.

The empty seat next to me made me think of Kailey. I wondered if she was on a job right now, putting a bullet in some poor bastard's head. Then I thought about Malinda. I wondered if she was with Kailey. After seven years, I still couldn't believe she had faked her own death. But that was the only way she could escape her past, she had said. The only way to protect me.

A stab of anger lanced through me, quickly followed by a wave of sadness. I took a deep breath of the salty air and shook my head. I couldn't think about them right now. I had a life to get on with. But that didn't lessen the pain.

The miles slipped by as Walter curled up on the deck beside me, the sun warm on our skin. We crossed the Gulf of Mexico in comfortable silence, my thoughts drifting as the autopilot steered us steadily toward El Cuyo. We were bucking a two knot current that runs from south to north. With that, we cruised at ten knots.

After letting the boat run on autopilot all night, while I snoozed in the wheelhouse, we now had five hours to go. The sun was casting a beautiful glow on the turquoise sea as it slowly lifted into the sky.

Walter and I enjoyed omelets for breakfast, then we prepared the boat for docking.

I snapped out of my reverie as El Cuyo came into view, a small fishing village on the southern coast of Quintana Roo in Mexico. Palm trees lined a white sand beach, and colorful houses were clustered around a main street running parallel to the shore. Fishing boats bobbed in the turquoise waters of the bay.

Walter barked and jumped up, pacing in front of the helm. I patted his head and adjusted our course, bringing the boat into the bay toward the marina.

As we docked, two young boys ran to catch the lines. They expertly tied the boat off.

"Thank you," I said and gave them each ten dollars.

"Gracias, señor," one of the boys said.

"Gracias," the other said shyly.

When they saw Walter, they ran to him and started to pet him. He ate it up.

After docking, Walter and I made our way down the main street, passing open-air bars and ramshackle houses. A few locals nodded in greeting as we walked by, eyeing the strangers in their midst. I kept my hands loose at my sides, senses alert. If Malinda had taught me anything, it was to always be on guard.

We stopped outside a bar called La Sirena, the strains of mariachi music drifting through the open doorway. "This looks like a good spot to start, boy," I said, and Walter barked in agreement.

I walked into the dimly lit bar, the air heavy with the scent of tequila and limes. A few patrons glanced up as I entered, then looked at Walter, but quickly returned to their drinks and conversations.

The bartender, a heavyset man with a thick mustache, eyed me warily. I sauntered over to the bar and said, "*Una cerveza, por favor.*"

He grunted and slid a bottle of Sol across the bar. I took a long drink, surveying the room. What was I going to do for a week here by myself?

Chapter 4

When I returned to the marina, the two boys were still there. They came running to me. "Are you leaving now?" the taller boy asked.

"No, I'll be here for a while. I'll sleep on the boat."

"Watch out for Pedro."

"Who's Pedro?"

"He's a real bad hombre. He makes everyone pay him. Even us."

"What about your local police? Don't they protect you?"

"No, they are cowards. Pedro doesn't care about them."

"Okay, I'll watch out for him," I said and turned to go to my boat.

"They have taken Casey and Luke prisoner. Out there on their dive boat," one boy said and pointed to the sea.

That stopped me in my tracks. I turned and walked back to them.

"What are your names?" I asked the two.

"I am Mario," the taller boy said, then looked at his friend.

"Tito," he answered.

"Well, Mario and Tito, tell me about the two men who were kidnapped."

"Mister Casey," Mario said, "he owns the boat they are on. They're looking for *The Tide*. It's a treasure ship that sunk a long time ago."

"Two hundred forty years ago," Tito said.

"Tell me about Casey," I said.

"He is tall and handsome," Tito said, talking more now than he did at first. "He has a tattoo on his arm that says...."

"In me I trust," I interrupted.

"That's right," Mario said.

"Where is their boat?" I asked, looking out into the Gulf.

"There," Mario said, pointing to a speck on the horizon. *"Malinda's Star."*

The name went through me like a gunshot. There was no doubt that it was Malinda's brother out there, and he was in trouble.

"How many men were there?" I asked.

"Two in the tender with them but more on the boat already. There will be more come too. Pedro has a big gang. Mean men."

I knew my vacation was over now. I had stumbled into yet another case and it was larger than I could handle. But I thought I would give it a try before I called Malinda.

• • • •

I DECIDED TO RETURN to town and visit the local cafés and shops where the tourists go.

"Can Walter stay here for a while?" Mario asked me.

"Sure, I'll be right back," I said.

I asked the owners if they knew anything about Pedro. Some just shook their heads and walked away. But there were a few who eagerly talked about him.

I learned that not too many people in this village had ever seen Padro Diez. He was more like a ghost. Those who have looked upon him said he was a towering figure with a scar running down the left side of his face. He was known to enforce his will with a cruel and sadistic hand.

But he had a secret: a weakness for beautiful women. And when he laid eyes on Rosalinda, he was smitten. He had seen her at one of the local bars and had been following her ever since. Rosalinda knew of his obsession with her, but didn't share his sentiments. Pedro was determined to make her his. He was a tough man who would not hesitate to kill, but this woman turned his fearless demeanor into jelly.

• • • •

I NEEDED MORE INFORMATION, and there was only one person in town who might help me: the bartender at La Sirena.

I walked into the bar, and the bartender looked up at me warily. "Another beer?" he asked.

"No," I said. "I need information. I'm looking for a man named Pedro Diez."

The bartender's eyes widened, and he took a step back. "You don't want to mess with Pedro," he said.

"I know," I said. "But I need to find him. Do you know where he is?"

The bartender hesitated for a moment, then leaned in close to me. "I don't know where he is right now," he said. "But I know where his men hang out. If you're looking for trouble, that's where you'll find it."

He told me where to look for Pedro, but said not many people had ever seen him.

I thanked the bartender and left the bar, making my way to the outskirts of town where the seedy establishments were located. As I walked, I kept my eyes peeled for any signs of danger. I knew I was walking into a trap, but I had no choice.

I stepped into a small cantina where I could hear the music spilling into the street. The bar was lined with rough-looking men drinking beer. I knew there would be no tourists here. There were several empty tables, so I pulled a chair out and sat at one.

The sound of the chair sliding across the wooden floor caught the attention of several of the patrons. They turned and looked my way.

One man in particular kept staring at me. Finally, he set his beer down and walked to my table.

He leaned down. "Señor, I believe you have stumbled into the wrong establishment," he said, staring at me.

"Do they serve beer here?" I asked.

"Yes."

"Then I'm in the right bar."

He straightened up but kept his stare on me.

"Get out of here now," he barked.

This drew the attention of the entire bar. It was now quiet.

"Who are you?" I asked.

"None of your business. It is time for you to go."

He reached down with a thick, calloused hand and snatched at the fabric of my shirt. I reacted quickly, hooking my fingers around his wrist and yanking him forward. His chest cracked hard against the wooden table as he stumbled towards me. I grabbed hold of his long, sleek hair and slammed his face into the table. His body crumpled to the floor like a rag doll as two more burly men walked my way.

I stood tall, square-shouldered, and stared them down, looming in all six feet four inches of my self-made menace. They stopped dead in their tracks at the sight of me, then looked back at the man on the ground.

The bearded one spoke up from behind the bar. "Pedro's going to be mighty angry when he hears you laid hands on his brother here, señor."

"I had no choice. Is Pedro here?"

He didn't respond, just stared with cold steel eyes as if expecting something from me. "I take that as a no. Tell him I'm here to discuss *Malinda's Star*—I have an offer for him."

My heart was pounding in my chest as I turned and left the bar.

I walked back toward my boat. As I did, I noticed that there were several men watching me. I think the word had already spread down the street. I hoped I knew what I was doing.

Walter was waiting for me on the dock. The two boys were still petting him. One was scratching behind his ear. He barely looked up at me when I stepped onto the dock.

"Mister Cam. Did you see Pedro?" Mario asked.

"No, I didn't. Have you ever seen him?"

"No. Just his men. He doesn't come here."

"Where does he go?"

"He stays in town, I guess. When I hear they are coming, I go home. Bad men."

"I'm going to take my tender out to the *Malinda's Star*. I should be back in an hour."

"Can Walter stay with us while you're gone?"

"It's up to him," I said, stepping into my tender.

Walter looked up at me but didn't try to move, as if he had found a new home. The fact that the boys wouldn't stop petting him didn't make his decision any harder.

I pushed off and started the engine. "If anyone comes looking for me, tell 'em I went fishin'."

The boys waved and nodded their heads.

I headed out toward the dive boat. I lifted my binoculars first to see what lay ahead. I only saw the boat. No other crafts were around.

I had expected to see more men on board.

As I neared the ship, I called out, "Casey!"

A man walked to the railing and looked down at me.

"What do you want?" he called.

"Is Casey on board?"

"No."

"Are you Luke?"

"Yes."

"Where's Casey?"

"Who are you?" he inquired.

"Cam Derringer, Casey's brother-in-law."

The man brightened a bit. "Cam, Casey has mentioned you. Come aboard."

I maneuvered to the dive platform on the stern and tied the tender off. I climbed onboard where Luke was waiting.

We shook hands, and I asked where Casey was.

"They took him. Pedro's men said when I brought them more gold, they would release him."

"Do you believe them?"

"No."

"What do you mean by more gold?"

"We found a chest full of gold and jewels. When we brought it on board, they were waiting for us. A man named Saulo killed the guard they had sent first, took the gold, and left. They returned an hour later and took Casey. They said they would let him go when I brought them more treasure."

"Can you find more treasure?"

"No, I never dive alone."

I let out a heavy sigh. "Do you have another tank I can use?"

Chapter 5

We put on our tanks and masks, then slipped beneath the crystal blue water. Luke showed me where they had discovered a chest before, and I tied a marker balloon to the large rock that marked the spot for reference. The balloon rose quickly to break through the surface of the water while we searched around the area.

Luke worked his metal detector as I brushed my hand along the sea floor inches from where the chest had been found. Suddenly, something caught my attention. I dug deeper to discover two gold coins resting in the sand. They were covered in barnacles and other debris from their two-hundred-forty-year existence below the waves, but the recent hurricane must have shifted enough sediment to bring them within reach.

I waved Luke over and held up my bounty. He swam beside me with his metal detector, widening the search area even further.

Within fifteen minutes, we had found six more coins. We left the marker attached and went to the surface. We pulled ourselves onto the platform and opened the bag.

"My God," I said. "If we found this in fifteen minutes, what do you think we could find if we took the sifter down?"

"I knew there would be more treasure down there. Now we have to find a way to keep it and get Casey back."

I noticed the two dive propulsion vehicles secured to the starboard bow. "Do those work?" I asked, nodding toward them.

"Yeah. If you're thinking of moving the boat and using them to return, we already gave that some thought. I think it would work, but we never got the chance."

"What's to stop us now? You can tell them that you gave up on this site and are going to check a little further out."

"There is a Dutch ship that sank out there. We might even find a treasure or two around it. But how are we ever going to bring up this treasure without them seeing it?"

I gave that some thought. "We'll have to give them some of it to get Casey back. Maybe we can slowly move the rest to my boat. I can anchor out another mile or so."

"That would be a long process."

"Yeah, it would. But at least we'd have something."

"We need to make contact with Pedro," Luke said.

"I think I might have already arranged that. I sent him a message that I had a deal for him about *Malinda's Star.*"

"What kind of a deal?"

"I don't know yet. If we could find a few more of these coins, that might satisfy him."

"I believe you're playing a dangerous game," Luke said.

"Yeah, me too. I just didn't know what else to do."

We decided that I would go back to my boat for the night. Maybe Pedro would pay me a visit. It wouldn't be a visit I was anxious to have, but I had to get Casey back.

I tied up the tender, and Walter ran to me, his tail wagging furiously. He licked my hand and then ran back to the two boys he had spent the day with.

"Mister Cam!" Mario called.

"Pedro and his men came to see you. He and one of them are waiting on your boat."

My heart raced as I made my way to the boat. A man was standing on the aft deck, holding a short automatic rifle in his left hand. He saluted me with two fingers. I kept my eyes fixed on him as I climbed aboard.

Pedro sat at my table with a drink in his hand, beckoning me over. I poured myself a drink before taking a seat across from him.

"You are brave," he said. "First, you beat up my brother, and then tell my friends where to find you. Do you have a death wish?"

"We'll see who the brave one is," I replied coolly. "First, let's make a deal."

He downed his drink and signaled for another. His friend obliged.

"What's your deal?" he asked, leaning forward.

I smiled, feeling the upper hand.

He smiled at me and narrowed his eyes. "You are not in a position to give me an ultimatum."

"Actually, I am. But for now, we won't worry about that if we can make a deal."

I slammed five gold coins on the table, their dull clang echoing through the room. His eyes bulged with desire as he regarded them greedily.

"We need two things to get more of these," I growled. "First, we need Casey. He's the only one that can guide us down there safely."

"And second?" Pedro asked breathlessly.

"We need to search a much deeper spot–the Dutch ship that sank so long ago."

"Why? It's too deep and covered in sand," he said skeptically.

"It possibly settled on a shelf, we just have to find it. The treasure may still be there untouched," I explained urgently.

Pedro eyed me coolly over his glass before speaking again.

"Sixty-Forty," he declared smugly. "My ocean, my terms."

"Fifty-fifty and we get Casey," I shot back with steel in my voice.

Pedro's gaze hardened as he slammed his shot glass onto the wooden table. "Deal," he said gruffly, "But if you try to cheat us, we won't hesitate to come back here and end all of you."

"Deal," I replied, stretching a hand out for him to shake. He didn't comply, but eyed me suspiciously. His next words confirmed my suspicions. "And now, there is also the matter of you beating up my little brother."

"I let him off easy," I replied coolly. "I don't let anyone threaten me and get away with it."

The man seemed to be sizing me up before finally cocking his head in challenge. "I should kill you right now," he spat.

"You won't touch me," I answered evenly as I pointed to the luxurious boat that surrounded us. "This isn't your everyday treasure diver's boat—it belongs to a very powerful friend of mine who could easily make sure that you never come back this way again if I asked them to."

Pedro scoffed and waved a dismissive hand at me. "You have nothing," he spat again but this time with less conviction than before.

"So, do we have a deal or not?" I asked.

He silently stared me down for what felt like minutes before finally rising from his seat and throwing his glass into the sea. "Casey will be here tonight," he muttered darkly, turning on his heels. "Don't make me come back and kill him." With that, they left the boat.

I sighed with relief. I really did have an ace up my sleeve, but I didn't want Casey to know that his sister was still alive. I remembered the mixed emotions when I discovered her. My wife, who I thought was dead for five years, then she showed up one day on my boat.

Chapter 6

I fixed a sandwich and waited for Casey to show up. I hoped he hadn't been beaten to a pulp by the ruthless gang. Pedro didn't seem like a man that could be trusted.

I started to make a plan while I waited in case he tried to double-cross us and take the treasure.

I decided to call Brittany. I wanted to know if she was in the Caribbean or elsewhere.

"Cam?" she answered. "What's wrong?"

"Hello to you too."

"What's wrong?" she repeated.

"Nothing. Why would you even ask that?"

"Because you're calling me. I can't remember the last time you called and just chatted."

I tried to think back to the last time.

"Yeah, I can't think of a time either. Well, I didn't mean to worry you. I'm in El Cuyo alone and was just thinking about you."

"El Cuyo, alone? Why would anyone do that?"

"The brochures made it look inviting. Walter's enjoying it."

"Did you cruise there on *The Same Old Song?*"

"Yes, it was very relaxing. How have you been?"

"I'm good. I'm still getting the details taken care of from your last adventure in the mountains. Did you ever hear from your author friend again, Emily?"

"Not a word. She did send me her latest book. I was in it."

"So, what kind of book will someone be writing about your trip to El Cuyo?"

"Everything is fine here. I'm just a little lonely and want to talk to a friend. You're so suspicious of me."

"I have good reason."

"Where are you?"

"I'm at home enjoying the evening. I'm watching *Yellowstone*."

"Great show," I said absently.

"Cam, are you sure everything is okay there?"

"Yeah, I just wanted to tell you I love you."

"I love you too. Take care of yourself, and if you need anything, call me."

"You do the same. Good night."

"Good night, Cam."

When we hung up, I felt better. Even though she wasn't here, she was close by and wouldn't hesitate to come if I needed her.

She ruled this area and could make Pedro disappear if I needed him to. The main reason I called her is that if anything happens to Casey on my watch, she'll never forgive me. I feel like I should at least tell her about him and let her make the decision.

I decided I would give this a day or two, and if I thought I needed to let her know, I would then. I don't want to worry her for no reason.

I heard someone walking the dock. Was it Casey? I stood and walked to the railing. It was Mario and Walter.

"I brought your dog home," he said.

"I knew you wouldn't want to keep him after you got to know him," I said.

"He's a good dog. Can I see him again tomorrow?"

"We'll see. If I'm still here, I guess it would be okay."

Mario brightened at the thought of seeing him again. He stooped and hugged Walter, then asked, "Is Pedro gone?"

"Yeah, he's gone. Everything is fine."

"Good. Bad man."

"See ya tomorrow," I said as he left the boat.

He waved over his shoulder. Then I heard him talking to someone.

I glanced down the dock again. It was Casey. He didn't look any worse for wear. He smiled and waved at me.

"Come aboard," I said.

He stepped onto the boat, and we hugged. We had been good friends at one time.

"It's good to see you, Cam," he said.

"You too, Casey. It's been a while."

"Have a seat," I said, waving toward the table. "Wanna beer?"

"Yeah, I could use one."

I grabbed two beers from the fridge and returned to the deck. Walter was next to Casey with his front paws on Casey's lap.

"Just push him away," I said, setting a beer on the table in front of him.

He kept petting Walter, who didn't mind it a bit.

"Tell me about Pedro," I said. "Do you know where they are?"

"They're staying in a hotel at the other end of the town. Pedro has a few guys with him, but I think he's planning on leaving soon. I don't know where he's going."

"Did he hurt you?" I asked, concerned.

Casey shook his head. "No, he just wanted the treasure. I think he wanted it so bad that he was willing to let me go. That's why I could come back here."

Casey took a long drink of his beer.

"Do you think they'll come back?"

He shook his head. "No, I don't think they will right away. Pedro thinks you're too connected to mess with. I heard him talking to his men. What the hell did you tell them?"

"I bluffed him. I told him I had a friend who could make him disappear. It might work for a while, but we need to be vigilant. If we double-cross him, he won't hesitate to kill us."

Casey nodded in agreement.

"Let's get some rest," I said. "We have a long day ahead of us tomorrow."

We finished our beers, and then Casey retired to the guest cabin after calling Luke. I went to mine and settled in for the night.

It was almost morning when I heard the sound of a boat engine. I threw on some clothes and rushed out to the deck. It was Pedro and three of his men.

"What do you want?" I shouted as they drew closer.

"I have brought you help," he called back. "They are good divers."

He let his boat bump the dock as one of the men jumped out. They transferred two sets of tanks and a few bags to the dock, then pushed the boat away, leaving two men standing at the bow of my boat.

"Bring me my treasure," he said as he drove away.

I looked at the two men on the dock who were watching me. "We leave in ten minutes," I said.

They started picking up their gear and began bringing it to the boat.

We were going to have to make a different plan now.

Mario was waiting at the dock when I took Walter for his morning walk. "I'll walk him, Mister Cam," he said.

Walter started to wiggle with excitement.

"Alright," I said, handing him the leash. "I'll leave his water and food bowls on the dock with enough food for the day."

I gave him a few rules for Walter and bid farewell.

With the gear stored, we left the dock and cruised toward Casey's boat with the two new divers onboard.

I radioed Luke and told him to bring his tender to our boat and collect the gear and us.

It was a hot and humid morning and not a cloud in the sky—a typical day.

I dropped anchor about a hundred yards from Luke and we set about getting the gear together I thought we would need for the day.

Luke came alongside and climbed onboard. He hugged Casey and told him he was glad to see him back.

"I don't know how long I'll be back. Pedro is demanding we bring him some treasure. I think I'm just a bargaining piece."

Luke looked at the other two men. "Who are they?"

"Your new crew. Rodrigo and Cruz."

The men nodded at Luke. He nodded back.

Chapter 7

We stood on the boat, the gentle rocking of the waves beneath us. I could taste the salt on my lips from the sea breeze and feel beads of sweat forming on my brow. We exchanged tense glances, our common goal hanging heavy in the air.

The sun was a blood-orange disk rising low on the horizon as Luke held the tender for us to climb aboard. The gang members, their eyes hidden beneath dark sunglasses, watched him closely, guns tucked into their waistbands. I could feel their tension in the air, thick and heavy like the humid tropical breeze.

"Alright," Luke said. He threw a rope over and released it from the cleat. "Let's get you back to Casey's boat."

I jumped aboard the tender before Casey hopped aboard himself, followed by the two gang members. Their eyes never left us. As we motored out to the open sea, I thought how dangerous these men were, and their patience had limits.

"Look," I whispered to Casey, keeping my voice low enough that the gang members couldn't hear. "We need to come up with a plan. We can't just keep playing along with these guys."

"Agreed," he murmured, his eyes darting to where Luke sat at the helm. "What have you got in mind?"

"Alright," I said, my mind racing, trying to piece together a strategy that would buy us time and maybe, just maybe, give us an edge. "When we get back to your boat, we'll set up a diversion. I'll go with the gang members to search the Dutch wreck while you and Luke use the DPVs to search *The Tide*."

"Isn't that a bit risky?" Casey asked, concern furrowing his brow.

"Maybe," I admitted. "But it's our best shot at finding a treasure and keeping it."

"Okay," he said, nodding. "Let's do it."

Once onboard, I approached Luke. "I'm going to take the gang members to search the Dutch wreck. You and Casey will take the DPVs and search *The Tide*."

"Sounds like a plan," he said, nodding. "Come with me."

I stepped into the cabin with Luke. The two men were busy with their equipment.

He opened a drawer and pulled out a gold cross. It was still covered with barnacles. He handed the half-encrusted cross to me and said, "Hide this in your suit. You can find it down there as a diversion."

"Alright then," I said, glancing nervously at the two gang members who were standing on the deck watching the cabin intently. "Let's get moving."

Casey looked at their Jerry Rat DPVs sitting on the deck. "I want to make sure we have a full charge before we go in."

He connected the power cords to them and started a charge on the batteries.

"We'll go down when we get to the wreck. The two of you can come in when they're charged and start your larger perimeter search," I said. Casey nodded at me.

We stopped about a mile away from where *The Tide* had sunk.

"The Cuyo Cannons," Cruz said looking down at the water.

The Dutch warship had been dubbed that name because of the cannons that had been found in the area. It confirmed that the ship had met its demise right here and had gone straight down.

"Have you seen it?" I asked him.

"A few times. There's nothing there."

"According to legend, there's over fifty million dollars in gold and trinkets."

"I have heard that too, but I've never found any," he said dismissively.

As we split up, me with the gang members and Luke and Casey watching the gauges on the DPVs, I couldn't shake the feeling that we were playing a dangerous game. One wrong move and it could all come crashing down, leaving us at the mercy of these ruthless men.

But there was no turning back now. We were in too deep. All we could do was push forward, hoping that our plan would work and that we'd find the treasure before time ran out.

I plunged into the warm sea, the splash echoing in my ears like a death knell.

The gangster men flanked me as we descended into the deep. Rays of sunlight filtered through the water above, casting mottled shadows over the seafloor.

My heart pounded as we drifted lower. My heart pounded as we drifted lower. The men's eyes were sharp behind their masks, alert for any sign of gold. I kept my gaze forward, not wanting to meet theirs. Betrayal simmered in my gut like acid.

The pressure increased as we plunged deeper, the weight of the ocean pressing in on all sides. My ears popped, and I swallowed hard to equalize. At 75 feet down, the world was a different place.

My thoughts churned like the currents around me. What if the plan didn't work? What if Luke and Casey were caught? Would these men hesitate to kill us?

"Keep moving," one of the gang members said through his regulator, his voice distorted and garbled. I nodded, pushing aside my fear and focusing on the task at hand.

We swam forward, our fins propelling us through the water with powerful kicks. Schools of fish darted in and out of coral formations, their scales shimmering like jewels. A sea turtle glided by, its ancient eyes watching us with disinterest. But there was no time to appreciate the beauty of our surroundings. We had a mission to complete.

And then we saw it. The Dutch shipwreck, Cannon Cuyo, loomed before us like a ghost from the past. Its once-mighty hull was now encrusted with barnacles and coral, a testament to the ravages of time.

My heart raced as we approached. Was this where we'd find the treasure? Or was it just another dead end?

I pointed at my chest and signaled that I would check the port side.

They nodded, disappearing into the dark recesses of the ship. I swam around the wreck, my eyes scanning every inch for anything that might prove useful.

"Focus," I told myself, my breaths coming in short, measured bursts. "Find what you need and get out."

As I circled the wreck, I couldn't help but think about the blood that had been spilled over this treasure, the lives lost in pursuit of a fortune long gone. And now, here we were, diving headfirst into danger once more.

Please let this work, I thought, praying that our plan would succeed. *Please let us find a way out of this nightmare.*

"Cam!" Casey called out from behind me.

"Find anything?" I asked, glad to see that they showed up here before going to *The Tide*.

"No." Luke shook his head, feigning disappointment.

He was doing a good job for the benefit of the two thugs.

"Keep looking," I said, more to myself than to them.

It was time for them to leave us now and search *The Tide* for the treasure.

And then, there it was—a glint of silver, half-buried beneath the sand. A relic of the past. A clue. I crouched down, fingers scraping against the gritty wetness, and unearthed a small cross. The metal was tarnished and worn, but unmistakably Dutch.

I held it up, getting everyone's attention.

Eyes wide, his face inches away from the artifact, Luke gave me a thumbs-up.

They realized it wasn't the cross they had given me. There really was treasure down here.

I motioned to the DPVs. Time's running out. They grabbed the handles again and took off for *The Tide* while I had the attention of the two men. Their motors whirred to life, slicing through the shimmering waves. My pulse raced like a drumbeat, echoing the thrumming of the vehicles.

Chapter 8

"**S**tay safe," I whispered under my breath, praying they wouldn't encounter any danger.

As Casey and Luke disappeared into the depths, I knew I couldn't just wait for them to return. I motioned for the other two to start digging in the area where I found the cross. It would keep them busy for a while.

• • • •

MEANWHILE, FAR FROM the diversion, Casey and Luke maneuvered their DPVs through the treacherous underwater terrain. Their powerful lights pierced the murky darkness, revealing twisted shipwrecks and vibrant coral reefs. The thrill of the hunt pulsed through their veins as they searched for any sign of the long-lost treasure.

Finally, after what felt like an eternity, Casey's light caught something shimmering in the sand—a cluster of ancient coins, glinting like gold in the gloom. Luke gave a muffled cheer, bubbles escaping his regulator, and they exchanged a knowing glance. This was it; they were close.

Following the trail of coins, they soon stumbled upon what could only be the ship's safe. It's wood was darkened with age. The heavy lock securing it only added to the intrigue.

The safe was half buried in the sand and lying on it's side. They tried to move it but it was going to take more than just the two of them to get it up.

They high-fived each other and did an underwater dance in celebration.

They were running out of time, so they worked together to carefully cover it with anything they could find. Hiding the chest out of sight, they planned to return later with a line to pull it up to my boat.

· · · ·

THE WATER'S PRESSURE weighed on me, but I tried to keep my focus on the task at hand. I peered around, watching the two thugs dig industriously in their search for treasure. They were so engrossed in their work that they didn't notice the unease that prickled over my skin.

"Hey," Rodrigo grumbled through his regulator, "how much longer we gotta stay down here?"

"Until we find something worth taking back up," responded Cruz, his voice muffled by the equipment.

As they continued digging, I couldn't help but worry about Casey and Luke. Had they found anything? Were they running into trouble?

I decided to give the divers new hope and inspiration. I pulled the cross Casey had given me out, and half buried it in the sea floor.

I waited until they looked my way, then brushed the sand away and pulled the cross out. I looked it over then glanced at them. They were swimming toward me.

One of them took it from me and held it up in his headlight. He looked elated.

Suddenly, the beams from the scooter's underwater lights cut through the murkiness as they approached. Relief washed over me, mixed with a surge of anxiety. We had to wrap things up down here before our air ran out or the thugs grew suspicious.

I held my hand up, asking if they found anything.

They shook their heads, no, glancing at the two men.

Casey pointed at his tank and then the surface.

· · · ·

I AGREED, NODDING MY head toward the others.

We started our ascent, leaving the depths of the ocean behind. As we swam upwards, I found myself plagued by thoughts of what Casey actually found. I could tell there was something they wanted to tell me.

I pushed the questions aside, focusing on the rhythmic movement of my limbs as we stopped to decompress before breaking the surface. The sun's warmth welcomed us back to the world above, but I knew that beneath the waves, danger still lurked.

"Hey, boss," Rodrigo called out as we surfaced. "What luck. Maybe the stories about treasure were true."

"Yeah, maybe you're not searching hard enough," Cruz grumbled, clearly frustrated. "He found two crosses, and you found nothing."

"You found nothing too."

I was glad to see some dissension in the ranks. That might work to our advantage later.

"Alright, let's refill our tanks and head back down," I said, trying to hide my impatience. I needed to know what Casey and Luke had discovered, but I couldn't risk revealing anything in front of the thugs.

"Here, let me help you with that," Casey offered, reaching over to help me unhook my air tank. As he did, his hand brushed against mine. He whispered, "Safe."

We worked together in tense silence, refilling the tanks and checking our gear while the other two brushed the crust away from the crosses.

Casey and Luke recharged their scooters as we geared up. "We'll be along shortly," Casey said.

"Alright, let's go," I finally announced, eager to dive back into the depths and uncover whatever secrets lay hidden beneath the waves.

As we submerged again, I found myself swimming ahead of the others, feigning interest in a particularly dense patch of coral. I needed a moment to myself, a chance to plan our next move.

As we continued scouring the shipwreck, my thoughts raced with possibilities—the treasure that could be hidden in that safe, the danger we faced in retrieving it, and the knowledge that time was running out. The suspense clung to me like a second skin, threatening to suffocate me as I swam through the murky waters surrounding the Dutch ship.

Chapter 9

The moonlight flickered on the water's surface as I leaned against the railing of the boat. The salty breeze tugged at my hair and filled my nostrils, but my attention was fixed on Rodrigo and Cruz. They were hunched over a table near the bow, their faces illuminated by a dim lantern. I could see the sweat glistening on their foreheads, the tension between them palpable as they drank from the rum bottle.

"Rodrigo," I called out, raising my voice just enough to be heard over the lapping waves. "Which one of you screwed up the search today? We should have found more treasure."

Rodrigo shot Cruz a venomous glare, his knuckles white. "Yeah, that idiot can't do anything right," he spat.

Cruz bristled, slamming his fist onto the table. "You wanna say that to my face, *cabron*?" He stood, towering over Rodrigo, his eyes dark with fury.

"Enough!" I shouted, feigning annoyance while stifling the satisfaction rising within me. With those two preoccupied with their petty squabble, it'd be easier for Casey to slip away and mark the underwater safe on *The Tide*.

Just then, we heard the low growl of an approaching motorboat. My heart quickened, my grip tightening on the railing. As the vessel pulled alongside ours, I saw Pedro stepping onto our deck, flanked by a group of menacing-looking men. Their guns glinted ominously in the moonlight, casting long shadows across the wooden planks.

"Supper time, boys," Pedro sneered, eyeing us with contempt. "What are we having?"

We gathered around the table, the air heavy with unspoken threats. Pedro's men looked over the two crosses we had found earlier, their greedy fingers caressing the ancient metal. They handed the smaller cross to Casey.

"Your cut," Pedro grunted. "Find more," he warned, his voice ice-cold as he pointed a finger at Casey's throat. "Or I'll be back to cut off your head."

Casey nodded, swallowing hard, as beads of sweat trickled down his temples. He shot me a desperate glance, and I knew we had no choice but to play along—for now.

As I took a bite of the stale bread and gritty beans on my plate, thoughts raced through my mind like lightning. Tonight, we had to mark that safe without getting caught. And somehow, we had to find a way to outsmart these bastards before it was too late.

The taste of blood and salt filled my mouth as I bit the inside of my cheek, a reminder that the stakes had never been higher.

"You two, stop drinking that rum," Pedro spat at Rodrigo and Cruz. "I want you to be sharp when I return tomorrow for more treasure."

With that, Pedro bid us ado and left the boat with his men. I was glad to see him go.

· · · ·

LATER THAT NIGHT, AS the boat gently rocked beneath a moonless sky, I lay in my bunk, feigning sleep. My heart pounding, I waited for the right moment to carry out my plan.

"Cam," Casey whispered from the other side of the cabin, his voice barely audible. "You sure about this?"

"Trust me," I replied, my voice low and steady. "It's our only chance."

Silently, I slid out of my bunk and tiptoed across the creaky floorboards, avoiding the spots I knew would give away my presence. I could hear the snores and heavy breathing of Pedro's men, their dreams filled with thoughts of plunder and bloodshed.

Reaching the door, I paused, taking a deep breath before opening it just enough to slip through. The cool night air hit my face like a splash of cold water, causing me to shiver involuntarily.

As I crept along the deck, I noticed Cruz's diving gear piled near the railing. Carefully, I picked up his regulator, examining it under the faint glow of the stars. This was my chance to sabotage Cruz's dive tomorrow, ensuring he wouldn't be able to reach the safe and giving us the upper hand.

With practiced ease, I tampered with the regulator's mechanisms, rigging it so that it would fail when Cruz reached seventy feet below the surface. It wasn't something I was proud of, but desperate times called for desperate measures.

"Cam," Casey's urgent whisper reached my ears. "Someone's coming."

My heart leaped into my throat as I hastily replaced the regulator, praying that it looked undisturbed. I slipped back into the shadows, holding my breath as Rodrigo staggered out onto the deck, a bottle of rum clutched in his hand.

"Damn seasickness," he muttered to himself, swaying unsteadily on his feet.

As he lurched over the railing, retching into the dark waters below, I couldn't help but feel a twisted sense of relief. My secret was safe—for now.

"Let's get back inside," I whispered to Casey, my adrenaline still pumping through my veins. "Tomorrow, we dive."

And with that, we retreated to our cabin, knowing that our fates were now as unpredictable and treacherous as the depths we were about to explore.

I gave thought to our plan while I lay in bed that night. I felt bad about what would happen to Cruz when the regulator failed. It would be a horrible death. Then another idea came to me.

• • • • •

THE NEXT MORNING WHILE we were getting our gear ready, I looked at Rodrigo and said, "How are you feeling this morning? I saw you out here last night. You looked like you were sick."

"It was those fuckin' beans," he grunted.

Cruz gave him a look. "You drink too much."

As we were picking our gear up, I called to Cruz. "Is that regulator loose?"

He sat his tank back down and examined it. "What the hell? I checked that last night before I went to bed." Then he looked at Rodrigo. "You fucked with my regulator. You are trying to kill me."

"Now, come on, you guys. You probably just missed it last night."

"No way," Cruz said. "I checked it."

"I didn't do nothing," Rodrigo said.

"You tried to kill me," Cruz said and hit Rodrigo in the jaw.

He went down and lay still on the deck. "He won't dive with us today," Cruz said. "He might never dive again,"

My plan worked without killing anyone. I was glad to see it.

Chapter 10

The sun burned a hole through my skull as I checked on Rodrigo, his face swollen and purple from the fight they had. Cruz shot me a knowing glance, a twinge of guilt gnawing at the corners of his mouth. But he had to do it.

"Ready?" I asked Cruz'

"Let's get this over with," he replied, securing his diving gear.

I took one last look at Rodrigo, lying unconscious on the deck. His chest rose and fell in shallow, labored breaths. Hoping he'd stay out long enough for us to get the job done, I slipped into my wetsuit and fastened the straps on my fins.

Cruz and I exchanged a final nod before we plunged into the water. The sea swallowed us whole, pooling into the crevices of our suits. Our thoughts drowned in the silence as we descended deeper, the Dutch shipwreck growing larger in our sights.

Cruz breathed heavily through his regulator, bubbles streaming around his face.

We swam toward the shipwreck, the ghostly remains looming like an underwater tomb. Barnacles clung to its rotting planks, while coral sprouted from every gap like nature's own graffiti. The eerie beauty both fascinated and terrified me, but there was no time for sentimentality. We had a job to do.

"Almost there," Cruz signaled, his fingers trembling with anticipation.

"Stay sharp," I signaled him.

· · · ·

WITH PRACTICED EFFICIENCY, Casey and Luke lowered the DPVs into the water and followed in after them.

"Remember," Casey whispered to Luke, his voice barely audible above the sound of the waves. "We need to act fast."

"Got it," Luke replied tersely, gripping the handle of his DPV tightly. They glanced at each other one last time before preparing to take off for *The Tide* again, their movements swift and precise.

Casey's pulse quickened as they approached the sunken ship, the weight of their mission bearing down on him. If they succeeded, they'd be rich. If they failed...they shuttered to think.

"Focus," Luke urged, sensing Casey's unease. "We can do this."

"Right." Casey took a deep breath, steadying himself. Together, they dove down toward the safe, their DPVs cutting through the water like knives.

Upon reaching the safe, Casey wasted no time in tying a marker balloon to it with a mere five feet of line. Meanwhile, Luke secured a dragline to the safe, digging out around it to ensure a smooth extraction. Their movements were fluid and efficient, a testament to their expertise.

As they finished their task and swam back to the surface, both men knew that their plan was far from over. But so far, it was been working.

"Tonight," Casey said as they broke the surface. "We come back here and raise this thing to Cam's boat. We can use his anchor winch. Then we'll finally have what we need and we can get the hell out of here.

"Justice," Luke added, determination burning in his eyes.

And as long as Rodrigo and Cruz remained in the dark, they might just have a shot at pulling this off.

"Exactly," Casey agreed, giving Luke a nod of solidarity.

"We'll have to be careful," Luke reminded him. "One wrong move, and our whole plan could come crashing down."

"Trust me, I'm well aware," Casey replied.

Their return to the Dutch shipwreck was swift, the powerful DPVs propelled them through the water with ease.

As they rejoined Cam and Cruz, they exchanged greetings and updates, careful to avoid any mention of their secret side trip. With luck, they'd have the safe secured on *The Same Old Song* tonight, and their enemies would be none the wiser.

As they traversed the dark, eerie corridors of the shipwreck, Casey couldn't shake the feeling that they were being watched. He glanced around, trying to spot any signs of danger while maintaining the facade of a curious diver.

Amazing, Cruz thought, examining an old rusted cannon. *To think about the history that lies beneath the waves...*

• • • •

A FEW MINUTES LATER, we decided it was time to surface. I took the lead, followed by Cruz, then Casey and Luke brought up the rear. As we broke through the water's surface, the sun blinded us momentarily.

"Good dive," I said, wiping water from my face. "Now let's head back to the boats."

"Agreed," Cruz added. "But we didn't find any treasure."

As we swam back toward the vessel, I could see a mixture of relief and anxiety on Casey's face. They'd managed to stick to the plan so far, but tonight would be the true test of their resolve and resourcefulness. The stakes were high, and there was no room for error.

As we hoisted ourselves onto the deck, a sense of calm settled over us. For now, at least, the secret remained safe.

Rodrigo wasn't lying on the deck now. He must have moved inside. As I entered the cabin, I saw him standing at the sink, holding an ice cube to his jaw. "I'll kill that mother fucker," he spat as he threw the cube into the sink.

He started out to the deck, but I put a hand on his arm to stop him. "Give it a few minutes before you do anything rash," I said. "He might want to apologize."

"I don't care for an apology. I want to kill him."

"If you do, Pedro will kill you."

Rodrigo seemed to ponder that point. I debated whether to stop him or encourage him. It would be better for us if they were both dead. But then Pedro would think we had something to do with it. This is a no-win situation for all of us. Unless...

Cruz burst into the cabin. "There you are. I should have killed you."

"I didn't touch your regulator," Rodrigo said.

"Bullshit. We'll let Pedro decide what to do with a traitor."

I butted in. "If I were you two, I wouldn't say anything about this to Pedro. He'll think the two of you can't do your job. You're going to have to learn to live with this."

They stared at each other for a minute, then Rodrigo went into his cabin, and Cruz went back onto the aft deck.

I smiled to myself. It would distract them, worrying about each other. That would give us some freedom.

Chapter 11

As the evening fell, the sky bled into a deep crimson, painting the water with an eerie hue. Night diving was treacherous, and Casey knew the dangers: limited visibility, disorientation, and unexpected encounters with predatory marine life. But we had no choice; retrieving that safe from *The Tide* was our only ticket out of this mess.

"Cam, keep an eye on Cruz and Rodrigo," Casey instructed in a hushed tone, his voice barely audible over the sounds of the waves crashing against the hull of the boat. "We'll handle the rest."

"Got it," I replied as I watched him and Luke don their scuba gear and test their DPVs. The sleek devices would allow them to move quickly through the water.

"Be careful," I added, watching as they exchanged knowing glances before slipping beneath the surface without a sound.

Time seemed to slow to a crawl, each minute stretching into an eternity as I waited for any sign of their return. I strained my ears, listening for the telltale hum of the DPVs or the splash of bodies breaking the surface, but all I could hear was the blood rushing in my veins.

Suddenly, there was a faint noise in the distance, like the whisper of a ghost. I peered into the darkness using my nightvision goggles and saw Casey and Luke emerging from the water, their silhouettes barely visible against the black expanse. Relief washed over me like a wave, my muscles relaxing as they hauled themselves onto my boat a hundred yards away.

• • • •

"GOT IT," CASEY PANTED. He and Luke had attached a line to the safe, which was now tethered to the winch on Cam's boat. With a nod from Casey, Luke activated the winch and felt the tension in the line as it began to lift the heavy safe from the ocean floor.

"Good job," Casey whispered, wiping sweat from his brow.

"Yeah, easy does it," Luke replied, his voice barely audible. "Let's get this thing on board."

The boat strained against the weight of the safe. It stopped as a plume of smoke rose from the motor.

"Damn it," Casey muttered under his breath. "We'll have to use the tender hoist."

Without a moment's hesitation, they rigged the hoist and connected the line from the winch. As the safe rose from the depths, the tension in the air grew palpable.

• • • •

I DID MY BEST TO KEEP Cruz and Rodrigo distracted. I hoped they wouldn't notice the absence of their comrades.

I went to Casey's room, turned on some soft music, and then locked the door on my way out. In Luke's room, I flipped on a light and closed the door.

If Cruz or Rodrigo got up in the night, they would think Casey and Luke were in their rooms.

• • • •

CASEY AND LUKE WORKED tirelessly to maneuver the safe onto the deck using the tender hoist. Their movements were slow and deliberate, each motion calculated to avoid making any unnecessary noise.

"Keep it steady," Casey whispered, sweat beading on his forehead as he guided the safe onto the deck. The metal clanked softly against the wooden planks, and both men exhaled a sigh of relief––their mission accomplished, at least for now.

"Alright," Luke whispered. "Let's get this thing open."

Casey nodded and handed him a crowbar, his eyes darting nervously toward the boat where Cam was with Cruz and Rodrigo.

Luke wedged the crowbar into the rusty lock, and sweat dripped down his brow as Casey watched *Malinda's Star* from afar.

"Easy there, mate," Casey cautioned, his eyes glued to the lock. "We don't want them to hear us."

"Right," Luke whispered, his hands steady as he applied more pressure to the crowbar. The rusted metal groaned in protest, and I could see the strain in Luke's body as he fought against it.

With one final, painstaking push, the lock snapped open, and the safe door creaked ajar. Both men exchanged a silent nod of victory.

• • • •

"GOT IT," LUKE MOUTHED, looking toward me.

Jackpot, I thought.

Nice work. Relief washed over me. But our mission wasn't over just yet; getting the treasure safely out of here was another challenge altogether.

"Cam?" Cruz said from behind me. "What are you doing?"

I turned to look at him.

"I couldn't sleep," I said.

He glanced toward my boat. "Is everything okay?"

"Yeah, just one of those nights. Do you think we have a chance of finding any other treasures down there?" I asked, trying to take his mind away from me being out here. I was praying that Casey and Luke wouldn't make any noise.

"We have found two crosses. Do you really think we have found the only treasure there?"

I shook my head. "No, you're right. There has to be more treasure on the Cannons Cayo. I do believe we found the only treasure chest on *The Tide*. It wouldn't make sense that they would have more than one treasure chest."

"I was thinking the same thing. But we'll check it again one time before we leave our hunt. You never know."

I didn't like the idea of them looking around *The Tide* again. No telling what kind of evidence Casey and Luke left behind.

Chapter 12

The sweat dripped off the tip of Casey's nose as he carefully swung the safe door open, praying that it wouldn't make any noise. He and Luke were risking their lives for this, but it was now or never. The metal hinges groaned softly, a sound swallowed by the oppressive humidity surrounding them.

"Would you look at that," Luke whispered, his eyes wide with amazement as they took in the treasure before them. It was a sight to behold: ancient gold coins, their edges worn smooth by time, glinting seductively in the dim light. Beside them lay several delicately crafted artifacts––an ornate dagger with an emerald-encrusted hilt, a bejeweled chalice, and what appeared to be a solid gold idol of a long-forgotten deity. This was the stuff of legends, the kind of treasure people would kill to possess.

"Casey, there's something else in here." Luke's voice pulled Casey out of his reverie as he pointed to a small, yellowed piece of parchment wedged between two stacks of coins.

"Let me see that," Casey said, his hands trembled ever so slightly as he reached into the safe and gently extracted the note. Unfolding it, he couldn't help but feel a thrill of excitement as he read its contents. It gave the name of another ship, the *Santa Rosalie*, which had been rumored to carry an immense fortune in gold and silver. He knew the tales, but it had never been confirmed that the ship held any treasure when it sank thirty miles east of where they stood.

"Luke, do you know what this means?" Casey asked, his voice barely above a whisper.

"Is it... another lead?"

"Better. This note confirms the *Santa Rosalie* was carrying treasure. It's still down there, waiting for someone to find it."

"Jesus, Casey. We could be rich beyond our wildest dreams." Luke's eyes sparkled with the promise of untold wealth, and he knew that Casey shared the same thoughts, ambitions, and fears.

"First things first, though," Casey said, forcing himself to focus on the task at hand. "We need to get this treasure out of here and hidden on Cam's boat without anyone noticing. Then we can figure out our next move."

"Right, right," Luke agreed, snapping back to reality. He glanced around nervously, making sure no one had discovered their illicit activities. "Let's do this quickly and quietly then."

"Agreed," Casey murmured as they set to work, both of them acutely aware of the danger they were in. But the allure of the treasure—and now the *Santa Rosalie's* secret bounty—fueled their determination. They would either walk away from this as wealthy men or not at all.

"Keep an eye out," Casey instructed, his voice low and urgent. "We can't afford to be caught."

"Understood." Luke's eyes scanned the surroundings, his body tense and ready for action.

Once the treasure was securely bundled in Cam's towels they carefully carried it inside the boat, their hearts pounding in their chests.

"Alright, let's stash it in the bilges," Casey whispered. "No one ever goes down there."

"Good thinking," Luke agreed, his voice straining under the weight of both the treasure and the pressure of their situation.

They lowered the precious cargo into the dark recesses of the bilges, hiding it amongst the dank odors and damp atmosphere. It would remain concealed until they could retrieve it safely.

"Let's get rid of the safe," Casey said, wiping his brow with the back of his hand, leaving a streak of grime and sweat in its wake.

"Got it," Luke responded, and together they hoisted the now-empty safe over the side of the boat, watching as it sank beneath the undulating waves. They held their breath, waiting for any sign that they had been discovered. But the night remained eerily quiet, save for the gentle lapping of water against the hull.

"I'll go down and release the line from the safe," Casey said. "You keep an eye out."

Casey dropped into the water and followed the line to the bottom. He unwrapped it from around the safe, then pushed sand up around the safe so it would look like it had been there for a while in case someone saw it. Then he surfaced again.

"Alright, we're clear for now," Casey finally exhaled, a hint of relief flickering across his face. But he knew their work was far from over. The *Santa Rosalie* and her untold riches still lay waiting, and the danger they faced had only just begun.

"Let's get back to our bunks," Casey whispered, his voice thick with exhaustion. "We'll discuss our plan in the morning."

"Right," Luke agreed, his eyes never leaving the dark waters where the safe had disappeared. "Tomorrow, we change our lives forever."

• • • •

AS I HAD FEARED, I noticed Casey and Luke drop into the water with their scooters. I reached for the switch beside the door and flipped it up. The deck lit up. But it also blinded us from seeing out into the water surrounding the boat.

"Why did you do that?" Cruz asked.

"I want to fix a drink. I'm not familiar enough to do it in the dark."

"The bar is inside," he said. "Let's go in there and have one."

"Sounds good to me."

We went inside. I left the lights on, but Cruz stepped back out and turned them off.

I hoped the flash of light was enough to warn them not to come aboard yet.

"Beer?" Cruz asked.

"Sure."

We sat in the salon and sipped our beer.

"What will you do with your portion of the treasure?" he asked me.

"Do you really think if we found any treasure, Pedro would let us leave with any of it?"

"Some, maybe," he said, a little noncommittal.

"Do you like working for a man like that?"

He studied my face for a few seconds and said, "I don't have a choice. Where I come from, you are either the hunter or the hunted."

"But Pedro doesn't seem like the kind of guy who would be pleasant to be around."

"No, he isn't. That is, unless Rosalinda is nearby. Then he is all smiles and happy. But only then."

"Rosalinda? His girlfriend?"

"He loves her madly."

He was quiet after that for a while. We finished our beers, and I asked if he wanted another.

"No, we need to get some sleep. We have another big day tomorrow."

"I need to take my boat into the marina in the morning to get my dog and a few supplies," I said.

I could tell he was giving it some thought. I didn't think he'd go for it, but he said, "Don't be gone long."

"Maybe just an hour or two," I said.

Cruz looked down the hall and said, "Your friends are up awfully late. Maybe we should check on them."

I felt a twinge of panic. "They'll be okay. Where's Rodrigo?"

"He's asleep," he said without taking his eyes off the room down the hall. "I'm going to check on them."

He stood. As he moved toward the cabins, I looked around for something to use as a weapon. There was a flashlight sitting on an end table next to the sofa. I picked it up and followed him to the first room.

It was Casey's room. We could hear music playing, and the light cast a soft glow from under the door.

He insisted on opening the locked door even though I knew it was locked. He put his hand on the knob and turned it. The door came open. We looked in to see Casey reading a book.

"What's up?" he asked.

"We were just checking on you," Cruz said. "Get some sleep."

He closed the door and started to walk to Luke's door but changed his mind. "If they want to stay up, that's their problem," he said. "Good night."

He walked to his cabin, closed the door, and turned off the light.

I went back to Casey's room and knocked softly.

He opened the door and looked around behind me. "Is he gone?"

"Yeah. How..."

Casey pulled me inside and closed the door. He pointed at a window. It was a slider and looked just big enough to squeeze through.

"We got the safe onto your boat and managed to open it."

"And?"

"Jackpot. We emptied it and hid the treasure in your bilges."

"What about the safe?"

"Ocean floor."

"Good job. Now we have to get it out of here without getting caught."

"Have you ever heard of the *Santa Rosalie*?"

The name did sound familiar, but I couldn't place it.

"Maybe," said.

"You will."

Chapter 13

The soft hum of *Malinda's Star* filled my ears as Casey, Luke, and Cruz meticulously prepared for another dive to the Dutch shipwreck. The morning sun painted the sky with streaks of orange and pink, casting a warm glow over the deck. I could taste the salty air on my lips and feel the anticipation building in my chest.

"Cam," Casey called out, his serious eyes locking onto mine, "I'll take you to your boat now."

"Thanks, man," I replied, grabbing my duffel bag and stepping onto the tender. As we motored toward *The Same Old Song,* my thoughts raced through my mind like a hurricane. *What would we find in that wreck? Would it be worth risking our lives when we could get away now and be satisfied with what we have?*

"Hey, Casey," I said hesitantly. "You ever get a bad feeling about a dive?"

He glanced at me, his eyes shadowed by memories of past adventures. "Every time, Cam. But we do it anyway. That's what makes us who we are."

I nodded, knowing he was right

As we pulled up alongside *The Same Old Song,* I couldn't help but admire her sleek hull and proud lines. She wasn't just a boat; she was my escape, my sanctuary.

"Good luck, Cam," Casey said, shaking my hand firmly.

"Same to you," I replied, stepping aboard.

"Check out the treasure, but be careful that no one sees it."

"Will do."

I guided *The Same Old Song* into the marina at El Cuyo. *What if something went wrong? What if the others needed my help?*

I'm usually not this worried, but this is Malinda's brother. If anything happened to him on my watch, our relationship would never be the same.

"Cam!" Mario, the dock boy, called out, waving enthusiastically as he approached, Walter, my loyal dog, trailing behind him. "I have your best friend here!"

"Hey, Walter!" I greeted him, scratching behind his ears. He wagged his tail and licked my hand, his brown eyes filled with love and trust.

"Cam," Mario said, his dark eyes serious, "I really enjoyed taking care of Walter. If you ever need someone to watch him again, just let me know."

"Thanks, Mario," I replied, clasping his shoulder. "That means a lot."

As I watched him walk away, I couldn't help but feel an odd sense of foreboding. Was it just my imagination, or were things about to take a turn for the worse?

With Walter now on board, I couldn't shake the nagging feeling in my gut. I needed to check on the treasure hidden below deck.

"Stay here, boy," I instructed Walter, patting his head before descending into the belly of the boat. The air was thick and musty, and the only sound was the soft creaking of the hull as it rocked gently on the waves.

The bilges were dark and cramped, but I knew exactly where to look. Hidden beneath a hatch in the floor was our prized possession—the treasure from *The Tide*.

I opened the hatch, my hands slick with sweat. Carefully, I unwrapped the towel around it, revealing the gleaming gold coins and precious artifacts within. Just one careless mistake, just one person catching a glimpse of this, and everything would come crashing down around us.

I re-wrapped the treasure and slid it back into its hiding place, securing the floorboard above it. As I climbed back up to the deck, I focused on steadying my breathing, pushing the panic back down into its box.

Walter gave me a concerned look as I returned to the deck. He could always tell when the tension was building inside me.

"It's nothing, buddy," I lied, forcing a smile and scratching his ears. "We're just going to have to be extra careful from now on."

The tropical sun beat down on us, casting long shadows across the marina. In that moment, I knew that the stakes had never been higher. The pressure was mounting, and there was no room for error.

As we headed into town, sweat trickled down my back, a reminder of the oppressive tropical heat.

"Come on, buddy," I said to Walter, who sniffed at a pile of rotting fruit by the roadside. "We don't have all day."

The bar we entered was dim and cool, a welcome respite from the blazing sun outside. A ceiling fan whirred overhead, casting shadows on the worn wooden floor. I spotted an empty table near the window and took a seat, Walter resting at my feet.

"Morning, señor," came a melodic voice that seemed to wrap itself around me like a warm embrace. I looked up to see a stunning young woman standing before me. Her dark hair cascaded over her shoulders, framing a face that could've been sculpted by angels. Rosalinda stood out on her nametag—even her name tasted like honey on my lips.

"Morning," I replied, trying to sound casual. "I'll have the huevos rancheros and a cup of coffee, please."

"Right away," she said, her eyes lingering on mine for a heartbeat longer than necessary. As she turned to leave, I remembered where I had heard that name. Last night, Cruz told me that Pedro was in love with a barmaid named Rosalinda. I couldn't help but wonder if Pedro's obsession with her had more to do with her beauty or the mystery that seemed to cling to her like a second skin. Either way, this was dangerous. I should get out of here as soon as possible.

When Rosalinda brought my food to the table, she surprised me by sitting down across from me. Her gaze was focused, curious. It was unnerving, but also exhilarating.

"Mind if I join you?" she asked, and I shook my head no, suddenly lost for words.

"What is your name?"

"Cam," I replied like a schoolboy.

Her eyes brightened in recognition.

"Pedro talks about you," she said, her voice low and conspiratorial. "He says you're searching for something... Something hidden beneath the waves."

I replied, feeling the tension coiling in my gut. "We're just divers. Nothing more."

"Of course," she said, her eyes searching mine for the truth I refused to reveal. But sometimes, even the simplest of actions can have the most profound consequences.

"Perhaps we could meet again?" Rosalinda suggested, her voice hesitant but hopeful. "In a few days?"

"Maybe," I said, trying to ignore the warning bells ringing in my head. "Why not?"

"Good," she said, her smile as bright as the sun outside. "I'll see you then."

She went about her job waiting on other tables but kept looking toward me with the seductive smile that framed her full lips.

As Walter and I left the bar and ventured back into the glaring heat, I couldn't shake the feeling that I was being drawn deeper into a web of secrets and lies—but the further I went, the more tangled everything became.

"Come on, Walter," I said, steeling myself for what lay ahead. "We've got work to do."

Chapter 14

The water was still and murky, the only sound was the steady rhythm of their own breaths. Casey, Luke, and Cruz swam cautiously through the remains of the Dutch shipwreck, their flashlights scanning the dark recesses for hidden treasures.

"Imagine what we could find down here," Luke's voice crackled through the underwater communicator for the benefit of Cruz. "This could be our big break."

Cruz, ever the adventurer, decided to extend the parameter. He dipped his head, signaling his intent, before swimming farther away from the wreck. Casey and Luke continued their search, unaware that Cruz had turned toward the safe. Their flashlights cast eerie shadows across the twisted metal and wood, revealing secrets that had long been submerged beneath the waves.

Soon, Cruz stumbled upon the safe they had tried so hard to bury. It lay half-concealed beneath a pile of sand and coral. It's surface clean of algae and sea urchins.

He hesitated for a moment, his instincts telling him that something wasn't right. But curiosity won, and he brushed aside the sand and debris, exposing the safe in all its glory.

What would he find within? What dark truths lay buried beneath the ruined ship and the weight of the ocean itself? There was only one way to find out. With a quick glance over his shoulder, Cruz prepared to confront whatever lay hidden within the safe.

He swam back to Casey and Luke. He signaled for them to follow him. They exchanged a glance before complying, their curiosity piqued.

As they approached the spot where Cruz had uncovered the safe, Casey and Luke felt the dread they had hoped they wouldn't have to deal with. They knew there was nothing inside, but they couldn't let Cruz suspect that they'd already found it and emptied its contents.

They had to act as if this discovery was just as thrilling for them as it was for him.

"Can you believe it?" Cruz exclaimed through his diving mask, gesturing excitedly at the safe. "This could be the treasure we've been searching for!"

Casey and Luke exchanged another glance, silently communicating their need to play along. With feigned enthusiasm, they nodded in agreement, their hearts pounding in their chests. They had come too far to turn back now.

Together, the three divers began digging sand away from the safe, their movements swift and deliberate. The suspense grew as they neared their goal, the ocean around them seeming to hold its breath in anticipation. Finally, they had cleared away enough sand to reveal the safe's door in its entirety.

"Let's do this!" Luke shouted, gripping the cold, rusted handle. With one powerful tug, he pulled the door open. The safe was empty.

The moment hung heavy in the water, the silence almost deafening. Cruz stared at the empty safe, his face unreadable behind his mask. Casey and Luke exchanged a panicked look, aware that their deception was hanging by a thread.

"Maybe someone got here before us," Casey offered weakly, hoping to dispel any suspicion. But in the depths of the ocean, surrounded by the ghosts of the past, the truth had a way of refusing to stay buried.

Cruz, his eyes narrowed in suspicion, lingered behind for a moment to examine the safe more closely. He noticed some scratch marks on the hasp where a lock had once been, and similar markings on the edge of the safe where it looked like someone had pried the door open before they got there. Silently, he filed away this information, not saying anything to Casey or Luke. Their reactions had not gone unnoticed, and the seed of doubt sprouted in his mind. Had they already found the safe and emptied its contents?

• • • •

I LOADED MY SUPPLIES onto the boat and fed Walter.

"Alright, Walter, let's hit the water," I muttered, starting the boat's engine and steering us away from the shoreline. "We have one more stop to make before we return to *Malinda's Star*."

As we cut through the waves, I couldn't help but wonder what Rosalinda would have to say to Pedro about our conversation. I had a feeling she wouldn't keep the conversation to herself.

I finally arrived back at *MELINDA'S STAR*. The dive boat bobbed gently in the water, and I could see Casey, Luke, and Cruz climbing aboard.

"Hey, Cam!" Casey called out as I approached, trying to sound casual despite the tension that hung in the air like a thick fog. "We found something interesting down there."

"Really? What did you find?" I asked.

"An old safe," Luke chimed in, his voice slightly strained. "But it was empty."

"Empty, huh?" I replied. While I tried to keep my voice steady, I couldn't help but wonder if Cruz was suspicious of me.

"Yep," Cruz finally spoke up, his eyes narrowed as he studied my face for any sign of deception. "And it looked like someone had already been there before us. There were scratch marks on the hasp and the edge of the safe."

"Strange," I said, attempting to play dumb. "I wonder what could've been in there."

"Who knows?" Casey shrugged, his eyes darting between me and Cruz. "It's lost treasure now, I guess."

"Right," I agreed, nodding slowly. I knew I had to tread carefully from here on out, with Cruz seemingly onto us. The stakes were higher than ever.

"Anyway, Cam," Cruz said, shifting his gaze back to me. "We would like to search your boat."

"Search my boat?" I questioned, raising an eyebrow. "Why?"

"Better safe than sorry," Rodrigo chimed in, a cold smile on his lips. "Just to make sure nothing's been... misplaced. The safe was found right about here, where your boat has been sitting."

"Ah, I see," I replied. "Well, go ahead. You're more than welcome to search my boat. I've got nothing to hide."

"Good," Cruz said, nodding curtly. His eyes held a glint of suspicion.

Cruz and Rodrigo began their meticulous inspection of my boat, each movement deliberate and thorough. I stood by, watching them comb over every inch. The waiting was unbearable, but I had no choice but to stand there and hope they wouldn't find any evidence of the treasure.

Finally, after what felt like an eternity, Cruz and Rodrigo finished their search. They exchanged glances before looking back at me, their expressions unreadable.

"Alright, Cam," Cruz conceded, his voice low and even. "We are satisfied that there is no treasure on your boat."

"See?" I replied. "I could have told you that from the start."

"Indeed," Rodrigo said, his eyes narrowing ever so slightly. "But it's always best to be certain."

"Of course," I agreed, nodding. "No harm in being thorough."

Although they had found nothing, I couldn't shake the feeling that Cruz and Rodrigo were still suspicious. Their search had only bought me a little time--I knew I couldn't let my guard down for even a second.

As we moved on from the boat, I couldn't help but feel that the danger was far from over. The tropical paradise that once promised adventure to some and fortune to others now seemed to harbor dark secrets and hidden threats at every turn.

"Alright, let's get back to *MELINDA'S STAR*," I suggested, eager to put some distance between us and my boat.

"Si, let's go," Cruz agreed, gesturing towards the tender. We all climbed aboard, with Walter taking his place at the bow.

As we sped across the water, I tried to focus on the wind whipping through my hair and the salt spray splashing against my face. Anything to distract myself from the uneasy glances being exchanged between Cruz and Rodrigo. There was a storm brewing within our ranks, and I could only hope that we had enough time to secure the treasure and make our escape before it erupted.

"Here we are," Casey announced as we pulled up alongside *Malinda's Star's* hull. One by one, we climbed onto the deck, the tension between us palpable.

"Cam," Cruz said, his voice carrying an unspoken warning. "We've searched your boat, and we found nothing. But don't think for a second that our suspicions have been completely put to rest."

"Understood," I replied, my voice steady.

"Good," he said, his dark eyes boring into mine. "Just remember––in this game, trust is a luxury none of us can afford."

We all dispersed, each of us retreating to our own corners of the ship. As I watched Cruz and Rodrigo walk away, their menacing figures disappearing into the shadows of the cabin, I knew that my time was running out.

Chapter 15

The sun dipped low in the sky, casting a golden hue on the bar's worn wooden panels. Rosalinda wiped down the counter with practiced ease, her eyes flicking up now and then to catch glimpses of the patrons scattered about. The atmosphere hummed with muffled conversations, punctuated by an occasional burst of laughter.

"Rosalinda," a gravelly voice called out.

She glanced toward the entrance and saw Pedro, his imposing figure silhouetted against the fading sunlight. His eyes locked onto hers for a moment before he approached the bar.

"Pedro," she greeted him, trying to keep her voice steady. "What can I get you?"

"Nothing," he growled. "I hear Cam was here."

"Cam?" she feigned ignorance, her heart pounding. "Oh, yeah. He stopped by earlier."

"Did he say anything about me?" Pedro's eyes narrowed, searching her face for any sign of deceit.

"Uh, no," she stammered. "He just came in to eat."

"Damn it!" Pedro slammed his fist on the counter, making her jump. Without another word, he stormed out of the bar, his anger radiating off him like heat from a fire.

Outside, Pedro barked orders at one of his men. "Get the boat ready. We're going to *Malinda's Star*. I need to have a word with Cam."

Rosalinda's hands trembled as she watched them leave. What had she done? She didn't mean to stir up trouble between them. Her mind raced, but there was nothing she could do now. If she could have her choice of the two men, she would choose Cam, but that would never be possible. She would have to wait to see how this played out.

• • • •

AS I CLEANED MY DIVING mask and blew out my tank, my thoughts were on Rosalinda. Her nervousness when mentioning Pedro had unsettled me. Little did I know just how much trouble that single interaction would cause.

A soft buzzing sound caught my attention, and I looked up to see a small boat approaching *Malinda's Star*. What now? The sinking sun glinted off the water, momentarily blinding me––Pedro stood at the helm.

"Pedro," I muttered under my breath, trying to gauge his intentions. His face was twisted with rage, and I knew this wouldn't be a friendly visit.

"Cam!" he shouted as the boat neared. "You've got some explaining to do!"

Whatever happened next, I had to be ready. Was he talking about Rosalinda or the treasure?

Pedro stepped from his boat to the dive platform on *Malinda's Star*. He glared at me.

"You have been busy my friend," he said. "Rosalinda tells me you went to her bar to see her."

I was actually relieved that he was talking about my short visit with Rosalinda. I thought about just saying, "Yeah, that's what happened," but I told him the truth.

"Actually, I did meet her. I went to her bar for breakfast, and she waited on me. We chatted, but when she told me she was your girlfriend, I left."

"I don't believe you," he said, raising his fists.

I didn't see any way out of this. If I fight him and win, he'll only take it out on us later. If I lose...

He took a swing at me. He was quick, but I was quicker. I easily dodged the attempt on my chin.

"Are you sure this is what you want to do?" I asked him.

He didn't answer, only scowled and lunged at me again. I was ready this time, blocking his punch and throwing one of my own. He stumbled back a few steps, surprise briefly registering on his face before it was replaced with rage.

We traded punches, each trying to gain the upper hand. Our fight was fierce, neither of us willing to give in. The sun had long since set, but the light from the stars above lit our way. We fought on and on until finally, Pedro stumbled back, exhausted. He looked at me with a mixture of shock and admiration before saying to Cruz, "Get him!"

I stepped back, my feet barely keeping up with the adrenaline coursing through my veins. Cruz approached me slowly, his stance wary. Then I heard the distinct click of Casey's rifle being cocked behind me. I spun around in time to see Casey aiming the gun squarely at Cruz and Pedro. Cruz froze in place and stared at Casey, then Pedro. Rodrigo stumbled backward, away from them both.

"I see," Pedro panted, his chest heaving. "You're not as helpless as you look." He gestured for the other two men to follow him with a jerk of his chin and started toward the boat. Casey kept his gun trained on Cruz and Rodrigo until they disappeared into the boat. As it turned away from us, we could hear Cruz shouting angrily over the roar of the motor, "You have made a big mistake, my friend!"

We watched the boat leave until it was just a speck on the water.

"You okay, Cam?" Luke asked, concern in his voice.

I rubbed my chin. "I'll be sore in the morning."

"What happened to the treasure from the safe?" Casey asked me.

"It's out there," I said, pointing to the ocean. "I dropped it off on the way back here. I thought it would be better not to get caught with it."

"Cam, I'm sorry I got you into this," Casey said, sincerity in his voice.

"Yeah, it's okay, but I think we need to get out of here."

"What about the treasure?"

"I think the best bet would be to come back another time and get it. I have the coordinates. There's a marker balloon tied to it a few feet off the bottom."

"Can we get it tonight?"

"I guess if we take the tender. It's risky, though."

"I don't think Pedro will be back tonight," Casey said.

"He's not the only predator out there."

The moon rose high in the sky, casting a silver hue across the horizon as we powered the tender out to the spot where I'd sunk the treasure.

"I'm ready to get this over with," I said.

"Right there with you," Luke chimed in, gripping the edge of the tender, his knuckles white. We all knew the risks involved in retrieving the treasure, but desperation and greed had brought us this far. There was no turning back now.

We approached the coordinates on my GPS. With the moon casting its shadow, it stretched out before us like a dark finger pointing to the depths below.

"Here goes nothing," Casey said, cutting the engine. The sudden silence felt heavy, suffocating.

I took a deep breath, pulling on my dive mask and regulator. "Remember, stay close, watch each other's backs." My voice sounded garbled even to me, but they nodded in understanding.

All three of us slipped into the warm water, the current tugging at our wetsuits as we descended toward the murky seabed. The pressure increased with every meter, my ears popping painfully until I equalized them. The treasure, concealed in an airtight plastic container, lay beneath a rock ledge, exactly where I'd left it.

"Got it!" Luke called out, his voice muffled by the bubbles rising around him. Together we wrestled the container free, our movements slow and labored underwater. It seemed to weigh a ton, but we managed to secure it to the harness we'd attached to the tender.

"Let's go!" I urged. Every second spent underwater felt like an eternity.

Finally breaking through the surface, we hauled ourselves onto the tender, gasping for breath. "We did it," Casey whispered, his eyes wide with disbelief as he stared at the chest dripping saltwater onto the deck.

"Let's get back to *Malinda's Star* now," I said.

"Agreed," Luke replied, his face pale as he cast a wary glance at the dark sky.

"Be careful," Luke warned, his gaze lingering on me as they pulled away, taking the treasure chest to safely stow on *Malinda's Star*.

"Always am," I called back, though I knew better than anyone that wasn't true. As their boat disappeared into the darkness, leaving me alone on *The Same Old Song*, I couldn't help but wonder if we'd just made the biggest mistake of our lives.

An hour later, we pulled anchor on both boats and began our journey back to Key West.

"Home-free," I hoped as I sat at the helm drinking a Wild Turkey.

I glanced to my left again and watched *Malinda's Star* cut through the water. Casey and Luke were keeping up with me. We would be back in Key West in a few days.

The next morning, I watched the horizon, squinting against the blinding glare of the sun reflecting off the water's surface. My eyes scanned it, searching for anything out of the ordinary. It was then that I spotted it—a boat, fast approaching.

"Damn it," I cursed as I recognized Pedro's vessel.

"Pedro," I muttered, the name tasting like poison on my tongue. He and his men were relentless, and they wouldn't stop until they got what they wanted.

I grabbed the radio, my hands and quickly dialed in the frequency for *Malinda's Star*.

"Luke, Casey, come in! You need to listen to me!" I shouted into the receiver.

"Cam? What's wrong?" Luke's voice crackled through the speaker, filled with concern.

"Pedro. He's coming after us. Fast."

"Stay calm, Cam. We'll figure this out." Luke's voice remained steady, determined, even as I could hear the underlying fear.

"Be ready," I warned, my gaze fixed on the boat slicing through the water towards us like a predator stalking its prey. "They're not going to give up without a fight."

"Do you have guns aboard?" Casey asked.

"Plenty," I said as I headed below to gather a few of them. "How about you?"

"We have four rifles and a few handguns."

"I'll do what damage I can with my automatics," I said.

Malinda's Star was about fifty yards away from me. There was enough room for Pedro's boat to cut between us, keeping us from shooting for fear of hitting the other boat.

I could see Pedro was thinking the same thing as he aimed for the space between us. I cut port and closed the gap. He would have to either stay back now or come around to the side of one of us.

He chose to go to the far side of *Malinda's Star*. I could hear shots being fired from both boats. I cut my throttle, falling back and cutting around the stern of their boat. When I had Pedro's boat lined up with mine, I opened fire with my ACR. I saw sparks flying off Pedro's boat. He turned and fled from us again. They were in a much smaller and more maneuverable boat than either of ours, which gave them a bit of an edge. His three four-hundred horsepower engines gave him plenty of speed to outrun our advances.

Guns roared to life once again, echoing across the open water like thunder. Bullets flew back and forth as the three boats danced around each other in a deadly waltz. Pedro and his men were relentless, their gunfire unyielding and terrifyingly accurate.

"Luke, do you have a clear shot at their engines?" I yelled into the radio, trying to make myself heard above the cacophony of gunfire.

"Negative, Cam! I can't get a good angle!" he shouted back, frustration evident in his voice.

"Keep trying," I urged him, ducking behind the wheelhouse as bullets pelted the side of *The Same Old Song* like raindrops in a storm. "Casey, what's your status?"

"Still here, just barely," he replied, his voice strained. "I think I winged one of them."

"Good job," I encouraged him, though my heart raced with fear for his safety. "Hold them off as long as you can."

Walter had run into the cabin as soon as the first shot was fired. I was glad of that and hoped he would stay there. He's been in a few of these fights.

"Cam!" Luke's voice broke through the chaos, filled with urgency. "I've got a shot at their engines! Taking it now!"

"Make it count!" I hollered back, praying that this would be the turning point in our favor.

The crack of the gunshot was like a thunderclap, and I held my breath, praying that Luke's aim was true. An explosion boomed from Pedro's boat, followed by a triumphant shout from Luke. The engine had been hit.

"Got one!" Luke yelled into the radio, but his victory was short-lived. A hail of bullets suddenly rained down on *Malinda's Star*, catching them off guard. One bullet struck the fuel line of *The Same Old Song*, and I watched as thick black smoke began to rise from my beloved boat. She was crippled, immobilized.

"Cam, we have to get out of here!" Casey's voice was desperate and panicked. I knew he was right, but leaving my boat behind felt like abandoning a piece of myself. *The Same Old Song* had been my home, my sanctuary, for so long.

"Go! Get to safety!" I shouted back, knowing that there was nothing left for me to do but buy them time. "I'll hold them off!"

"Cam, no!" Casey protested.

Then I heard Pedro's boat come to life again.

"Damn you, Pedro," I muttered under my breath, gripping my gun tightly as I fired off round after round at the approaching men. They were at the dive platform and boarding *Malinda's Star* now, their cold eyes filled with vicious intent.

"Adiós, amigo," one of them sneered as he aimed his gun at me. I ducked down in the wheelhouse again.

"Casey... Luke..." I called into the radio. No response.

I watched as *Malinda's Star* headed back toward El Cuyo with Luke, Casey, and the treasure while I was dead in the water, helpless to save them. Walter must have sensed that the war was over. He came out of the cabin and bound toward me. He sniffed around me, checking for blood. There was none.

I took the fire extinguisher from it's hold and ran toward the smoke. There was a ruptured fuel line and an electronic box riddled with holes. I doused them good with the foam and shut the fuel valve off.

I examined the damage. It wasn't good. I thought I might have enough parts on board to jerry-rig something to make it work long enough to get to land.

Walter and I walked back to the rear deck and looked to the horizon. *Malinda's Star* was about to disappear in the distance. What fate would Casey and Luke have in their future now?

I knew I was going to have to make that dreaded call.

Chapter 17

The sun beat down relentlessly on the deck of *Malinda's Star,* casting a cruel glare on Casey and Luke as they sat, hands bound behind their backs. Sweat trickled down their foreheads, stinging their eyes. The ropes dug into their wrists, the rough fibers chaffing the skin raw. Casey could feel Luke's labored breathing next to him, every exhale a reminder of his worsening condition.

"Such a shame, amigos," Pedro sneered, pacing back and forth in front of them. His thick Mexican accent dripped with malice. "We could have all been rich together, but now you lose everything."

"Go to hell," Casey spat, squinting up at him through the harsh sunlight. Pedro just laughed, the sound grating on his nerves like nails on a chalkboard.

"Your friend Cam, he will come for you, *sí*?" Pedro taunted, looking out towards the horizon where *The Same Old Song* was miles away, just a speck in the distance. "But it won't matter. By the time he gets here, the treasure will be ours."

"Cam won't let you get away with this," Casey growled, feeling a mixture of anger and helplessness rise within him.

"Really? And what can he do, huh?" Pedro leaned in close, his breath hot against Casey's face. "You two are tied up, your boat is mine, and your precious treasure–soon to be mine.

"Over my dead body," Casey snarled, the words tasting bitter in his mouth.

"Perhaps that can be arranged." Pedro straightened, a wicked grin spreading across his face. "But first, let's see if we can make a deal with your friend Cam."

Casey's heart pounded in his chest, each thud echoing the fear and desperation that threatened to consume him. He had to find a way to warn Cam before it was too late. But with his hands bound and Pedro's men watching their every move, escape seemed impossible.

He glanced over at Luke, whose shallow breaths filled the oppressive silence between them. A trickle of blood dripped down Luke's side.

"Stay strong, Luke," he whispered, hoping he could hear. "We'll find a way out of this."

As Pedro turned away, Casey's mind raced with possibilities, each more dangerous than the last. But he knew one thing for sure: he couldn't give up without a fight. The treasure was theirs by right, and if Pedro thought they would just hand it over, he had another think coming.

"Luke," Casey whispered urgently. "You still with me, buddy?"

"Y-yeah," Luke managed to choke out, his voice barely audible over the sound of the waves crashing against the hull of *Malinda's Star*. He looked down at the blood seeping through the makeshift bandage on his side, pain etched across his face. "But I don't know for how much longer."

"Stay focused, we'll get you help," Casey reassured him as he scanned their surroundings for any opportunity.

Pedro barked orders to his crew, who busied themselves preparing to anchor the yacht. The tension among them was palpable, and Casey knew they had to act fast. As the anchor dropped into the water, Pedro ordered two of his men to take the tender into the marina at El Cuyo.

"Let's go," Pedro commanded, pulling Casey and Luke to their feet and toward the tender. "Time to pay a little visit to our friend Cam. He'll be here soon."

As they approached the dock, the roar of an engine in the distance caught Casey's attention. Could it be Cam? *No, it's too soon.*

"Pedro," Casey said, trying to keep his voice steady despite the fear clawing at his chest. "If you let us go now, we can all walk away from this. You don't have to do this."

"Nice try," Pedro scoffed, studying Casey's face for any sign of weakness. "But I'm not letting you or your friend go until I have every last piece of that treasure."

Casey clenched his jaw, anger bubbling beneath the surface. They were running out of time, and he knew it. But one thing was certain: he wasn't going to let Pedro win without a fight.

As the tender pulled up to the dock, Tito and Mario saw Pedro and his men approaching. They exchanged nervous glances, sensing that something was wrong. As they tied off the tender, Mario noticed Luke's pale face and the blood staining his shirt.

"Señor," Mario said urgently, addressing Pedro. "This man is hurt. He needs a doctor."

Pedro's eyes flicked to Luke, then back to Mario, a cruel smile playing on his lips. "Does he now?" he asked mockingly. "Well, if you're so concerned, then you find him a doctor."

He turned to his men, jerking his head towards Casey. "Take this one with us. We're not leaving any loose ends."

Tito and Mario shared a worried look as Pedro and his men led Casey away, leaving them alone with the injured Luke. The boys glanced at the retreating group, then at each other, determination filling their eyes.

"Stay with him, Tito," Mario instructed, his voice trembling slightly. "I'll go find help."

"Be careful," Tito whispered, watching as Mario took off running down the docks.

As the sounds of Pedro's laughter echoed in the distance, Casey's heart raced. He knew that Luke's life hung in the balance, and it was up to him to find a way out of this mess.

"Wait!" Mario called out, his voice carrying across the distance. Pedro stopped, turning to face him with a raised eyebrow.

"Speak, boy," Pedro sneered, his grip still tight on Casey's arm.

"Señor Pedro," Mario began, trying to keep his voice steady. "If Cam shows up here, what should I tell him?"

"Cam?" Pedro scoffed, a sinister grin spreading across his face. "You can tell him that he can have his friend, Casey, back when we get all the treasure."

With that, he shoved Casey forward, and they continued their march away from Luke and the boys.

As Pedro's taunting words reverberated in Casey's ears, a surge of hope flickered inside him. He knew Cam was resourceful, and if there was one thing that could tip the scales in their favor, it was the treasure. A plan began to form in his mind, one that might just save them all.

"Pedro," Casey said, his voice strained but steady. "You're making a mistake. The treasure... you'll never find it."

"Really?" Pedro replied with a vicious smile, tightening his grip on Casey's arm. "And where would it be, then?"

"You'll have to find out for yourself," Casey shot back, gritting his teeth against the pain.

"Bold words," Pedro said, his eyes narrowing. "But they won't save you, amigo."

He pushed Casey along, leaving him with no choice but to follow. But as he walked, Casey clung to the hope that somehow, someway, Cam would come through for them and turn the tables on Pedro and his men. All he had to do now was survive long enough for that moment to come.

Chapter 18

I stepped onto the deck and surveyed my battered boat. The salty sea wind whipped at my face, stinging the cuts on my cheeks. Gunshots peppered the hull like a cruel tattoo, leaving multiple holes in their wake.

"Damn," I muttered under my breath, running my fingers over the jagged edges. Most of them appeared superficial, but I knew better than to underestimate the damage. A quick examination revealed that the gas line had been hit, and some electronics were fried. The boat was crippled, but not beyond repair.

It was crucial I got everything fixed before anyone else came snooping around.

Taking out a small, weathered notebook from my pocket, I scribbled a list of the necessary repairs and materials. The ink smudged against the damp pages, but the words remained legible—if only barely. With every item crossed off, I felt a little more in control. There was one name however, I hesitated to write down: Malinda.

"Can't involve her," I whispered to myself. She was not to be dragged into this mess. Not again. Not unless there was no other choice. Instead, I dialed Jack's number, knowing he'd have my back, even if it meant getting his hands dirty.

"Jack, it's Cam," I said when he answered, my voice low and tense. "Listen, I'm in a bit of a bind here. I need your help."

"Cam?" Jack replied, sounding both concerned and unsurprised. "What's happened this time?"

I explained the whole mess to him. I told him about Casey and that the last time I saw him, Pedro was hauling him away in Casey's boat. "But I need you to get me some things for my boat—a new gas line and some electronics," I told him where I was about two hundred miles from Key West.

"Two hundred miles?"

"Yeah."

"I'll call Pete. He owes me. We'll fly to you on his seaplane. Once we get your boat going, he can leave. I'm staying with you."

"You don't have to do that. It's not safe here."

"Sure thing, Cam. But, one more thing, have you considered calling Malinda? She might help." Jack's suggestion made me wince; he knew her situation better than anyone.

"Jack, not now. Just...not yet. I don't want to put her in danger unless absolutely necessary." My grip tightened on the satellite phone as I spoke, the smooth plastic becoming slick with sweat. "Please, just do what you can for me. I'll handle the rest."

"Alright, Cam. You've got it. I'll get everything together and meet you there. Just... be careful, okay?"

I gave him my coordinates.

"Thanks, Jack. I owe you one." I hung up the phone and let out a long, slow breath.

As I paced around *The Same Old Song*, my fingers traced over the bullet holes in her hull, each one a reminder of how close I'd come to meeting my end. My thoughts turned back to Malinda, and I couldn't help but feel a pang of guilt for keeping her in the dark. It was better this way, safer, but it didn't make it any easier. She'd been through enough already.

Walter sensed my unease and pressed close to my side, whining softly. I reached down to pet him, his fur soft and warm beneath my fingers. "Don't worry, buddy," I murmured. "We'll get out of this."

The tropical sun blazed overhead, casting shimmering heat waves on the ocean's surface. I could almost taste the salt in the air as I squinted against the bright light, scanning the horizon for any sign of danger.

But for now, all I could do was wait. Wait for Jack, for the parts I needed, and pray that Casey would be safe.

As the day wore on, the tension grew unbearable. Walter paced restlessly, and I found myself doing the same. Despite the heat, a chill settled deep in my bones, a constant reminder that time was of the essence and that death lurked just beyond the horizon.

Finally, unable to bear the oppressive atmosphere any longer, I decided to take Walter for a swim off the swim platform. It was a risk—with Jack still nowhere in sight and our safety uncertain, leaving *The Same Old Song* even briefly felt like tempting fate. But I needed to clear my head, and Walter's increasing restlessness was driving me mad.

"Alright, boy," I said, forcing a smile. "Let's take a break, shall we?" Walter's ears perked up at the suggestion, and he wagged his tail eagerly as I led him to the swim platform. I scanned the surrounding water one last time for any signs of sharks, but all seemed calm.

"Okay, here goes nothing," I muttered under my breath, and together, Walter and I plunged into the blue water.

Though the water was warm, the shock of it against my heated skin was invigorating, washing away some of the tension that had been building throughout the day. Walter paddled around me, barking happily, his spirits lifted by the impromptu swim. For a moment, as we drifted in the water together, it was almost possible to forget the danger we were in, the deadly game of cat and mouse we'd become unwilling participants in.

But all too soon, reality came crashing back. Treading water, I glanced towards *The Same Old Song*, its bullet-ridden hull a stark reminder of the events that had brought us here. With a weary sigh, I called Walter back to me. "Come on, boy. Time to get out."

Reluctantly, we clambered back onto the swim platform, our wet clothes and fur clinging to our bodies. I fired up the grill and cooked some steaks, the rich aroma of the meat filling the air. Walter sat beside me, drooling in anticipation, and for a moment, we were just a man and his dog, adrift on the open ocean.

"Here you go, boy," I said, tossing him a juicy piece of steak. He caught it midair, devouring it in seconds. As I took a bite of my meal, I knew that this brief respite couldn't last. Soon, night would fall, and with it, the promise of more danger and more uncertainty.

Chapter 19

The morning was still young when I woke up, feeling the heat already starting to build. Sweat clung to my skin as I pulled myself off the bunk, groaning at the stiffness in my limbs. Walter whined from his spot on the floor, his tail thumping against the wooden planks.

"Alright, buddy," I muttered, bending down to scratch behind his ears. "Let's get you some breakfast."

I opened a can of dog food and dumped it into Walter's bowl, the familiar smell making me cringe. As he dug in, I surveyed the damage from last night's encounter. Bullet holes peppered the hull like a swarm of angry bees had attacked. With a sigh, I grabbed a fiberglass repair kit and began patching the holes, the resin stinging my nostrils.

"Damn vacation," I mumbled, wiping sweat from my brow. What was supposed to be a peaceful escape had quickly turned into a nightmare. The sea breeze had brought trouble and danger instead of serenity.

Walter's sudden barking snapped me out of my thoughts. His head was raised, ears perked, and tail stiff. I strained my ears, but all I could hear was the gentle lapping of water against the boat.

"Easy, boy. What is it?" I asked, following his gaze out to the horizon.

A small airplane cut through the sky, its engine roaring above the ocean's waves. My heart raced as it approached. If it was them, I'd have backup. If it was someone else, we were sitting ducks.

The plane dipped lower, landing on pontoons fifty yards away. It taxied closer, and I finally made out the familiar faces of Jack and Pete in the cockpit.

"About damn time," I called out, grinning as they climbed aboard.

"Cam, how the hell did you get into all this mess?" Jack asked, looking around at the bullet holes and damage. His eyes were full of concern, but there was a hint of amusement lurking in their depths.

"Long story," I replied. "I just wanted some peace and quiet, you know? But apparently, that's too much to ask for."

"Seems like it," Jack chuckled, patting me on the back. "Well, let's get to work then. We'll get you out of this mess."

For the next two hours, we worked tirelessly on the boat repairs. Jack and I patched up the remaining holes while Pete tinkered with the engine, his expertise invaluable. The sun beat down on us, but we didn't stop, determined to make the boat seaworthy again.

As I sanded down the last patch, my hands ached and sweat dripped from my brow. There was an odd sense of satisfaction in repairing the damage, reclaiming a small slice of control in a situation that had spiraled beyond my grasp.

Finally, after what felt like an eternity, the boat was repaired. I turned the key in the ignition, and the engine roared to life. A smile spread across my face as I looked at Jack and Pete, grateful for their help.

"Thanks, guys," I said, my voice hoarse from the effort. "I don't know what I would have done without you."

"Anytime, Cam," Jack replied, clapping me on the shoulder. "Now, let's get out of here and put this mess behind us."

"Sounds like a plan," I agreed, my eyes scanning the horizon for any signs of trouble. I couldn't shake the nagging feeling that we were being watched, but I pushed it to the back of my mind. Paranoia wasn't going to help us now.

"Alright, I'm heading back to Key West," Pete announced, adjusting his pilot's cap. "You guys take care. And Cam, if you need anything, don't hesitate to call."

"Will do, Pete. Thanks again," I responded, offering him a firm handshake. He nodded and climbed into his plane, disappearing into the cockpit.

Jack and I watched as Pete taxied away from the boat, the propeller slicing through the air with a deafening roar. The seaplane lifted off the water's surface, ascending into the clear blue sky. Within moments, it had become nothing more than a tiny speck against the vast expanse above.

"Alright, let's get moving," Jack said, turning to me. "Next stop: El Cuyo."

"Jack, did you mention any of this to Diane?"

"Sorry, Cam, I had to. That reminds me, I should call her."

"Tell her we're fine and not to worry."

"I will. Don't you want to talk to her?"

"I don't think I should. I don't feel like being yelled at."

Jack laughed. "Her bark is worse than her bite. You keep the boat steady. I'll be right back."

I nodded, gripping the wheel tightly as I steered the boat toward our destination. The motor hummed beneath us, a reassuring sound amidst the uncertainty we faced.

As we made our way across the glistening sea, my thoughts raced with potential scenarios, each more dangerous than the last. What awaited us on the other side? Would we find answers or merely dig ourselves deeper into trouble?

The boat cut through the waves, leaving a frothy trail in its wake as we ventured further from safety and deeper into the unknown.

"Hey, Cam," Jack called out from the back of the boat, his brow furrowed as he fiddled with some equipment. "How much fuel we got left?"

"Enough to get us there, I hope," I replied, trying to sound more confident than I felt. The needle on the gauge rested precariously close to empty.

"Better hope so," Jack grumbled, wiping sweat from his brow with the back of his hand. "We don't need any more trouble right now."

"Tell me about it," I said, my grip on the wheel tightening. This vacation had turned into anything but a relaxing getaway, and now our lives hung in the balance.

"Cam." Jack's voice pulled me back from the brink. "How much fuel did you lose out there?"

"Not much. The gauge is probably broken. I had enough to reach Key West."

"And you were halfway there. Halfway back equals all your fuel."

"We'll make it. I had extra."

"Almost there," I whispered, more to myself than Jack.

"Damn straight," he replied, clapping me on the shoulder. "And we'll get through this, Cam. Together. We won't let Casey or Malinda down. Even though hopefully, she'll never know about it."

"Here goes nothing," I said.

I never felt this way before. I'd been in plenty of hot situations, but this time, my relationship with Malinda was at risk. It was almost too much for me to bear.

Chapter 20

The sun burned hot on the horizon as we approached the dock. Sweat trickled down my spine, adding to the dampness of my shirt. Mario and Tito stood waiting, their eyes fixed on our boat with an intensity that made my heart race. The tension in the humid air was palpable.

I guided the boat toward the dock. My hands were steady. We bumped the dock with a soft thud, and I threw the lines to Mario and Tito. Their movements were swift and efficient as they tied us off.

"Pedro says he'll return Casey once you hand over the treasure," Mario blurted out excitedly.

"Where's Pedro now?" I asked.

"Don't know," Mario shrugged, his gaze never leaving mine. "But he left Luke here for us to find a doctor."

"Is Luke okay?" My voice cracked from the dryness of my throat. Luke was more than just part of our crew; he was like family to me now.

"Found him a doctor and took him to Centro De Salud El Cuyo," Tito chimed in, his eyes darting between Jack and me. "He's alive, at least."

"Thanks for that," I spat, not bothering to hide my contempt. "Pedro better keep his end of the bargain."

"Can you get the treasure first?" Mario asked. "Then they will talk about deals."

We needed to find Pedro and get Casey back, but first, we'd have to give up everything they had worked so hard for, but there was no other way.

It would be better to have them back safely than to have their treasure.

"Let's get this over with," I said. "I don't suppose you boys would like to keep an eye on Walter again?"

"Si, we will do it," Mario said excitedly. They ran to the boat and started petting him. He lay down so they could get to his belly. What a ham.

"Mario." He looked at me. "Can you fuel my boat up?"

"*Si*, Mister Cam," he said and ran to the pumps.

"Come on, Jack. We need to see Luke," I said. "If anyone has any clues about Pedro's whereabouts, it's him."

"Agreed," he replied, his muscles tensing with anticipation.

The clinic was only four blocks from the marina, but it felt like miles away.

As we approached Centro De Salud El Cuyo, the sterile white walls of the clinic stood in stark contrast to the vibrant colors of the town. The doors slid open, releasing a wave of cold, sanitized air that sent shivers down my spine.

"Cam," Luke croaked as we entered his room. He looked pale and weak, but the fire in his eyes remained undimmed. "You shouldn't be here."

"Where else would we be?" I asked, offering a weak smile as I gripped his hand. "We're not leaving without you or Casey."

I introduced Jack to Luke.

"Do you know where we can find Pedro?" Jack asked.

"Pedro..." Luke winced, pain etched across his face. "I don't know where he hangs out. I'm sorry."

"Hey, don't worry about it," I reassured him, trying to sound confident despite the odds. "I know where Pedro hangs out. It's at the other end of town, where all the seedy bars are."

"Are you sure?" he asked, raising an eyebrow. "How'd you find that out?"

"Let's just say I've been around," I replied cryptically. "We've got to move fast if we want to catch him."

"Be careful," Luke whispered as we left the room, his grip on my hand tightening for a moment before letting go. "Pedro is dangerous."

"Trust me," I whispered back. "We're not going to let him win."

As Jack and I left the clinic, I felt a sudden urge to make a pit stop. "Hey, Jack," I said, pausing mid-stride. "I think we should drop by Rosalinda's bar before we track down Pedro. She might have some useful information."

"Good idea," Jack replied, his eyes scanning the crowded streets as if he already sensed danger lurking around every corner.

We hurried through the lazy town, the air thick with the scent of grilled fish, gasoline, and sweat. The sun was almost gone, casting long shadows as we made our way to Rosalinda's bar.

The moment we entered, the sultry atmosphere enveloped us like a second skin. A slender woman with dark hair piled high on her head stood behind the counter, wiping glasses with an air of regal grace. It was Rosalinda.

"Cam," she greeted me warmly, her voice low and throaty. "What brings you here today?" She turned and smiled at Jack, taking in his six-foot-five frame of muscle.

"Jack, this is Rosalinda," I said.

She placed her hand on his arm. "Hello, Jack," she said in her sultry voice.

"Rosalinda," he said.

"Pedro," I said without hesitation. "We need to find him. Have you seen him recently?"

"Ah, *sí*," she replied, her gaze narrowing ever so slightly. "He was here about an hour ago, bragging to anyone who would listen. He said he was going to be rich.

"He told me he was going to Loncheria El Amigo Willy's to get some fish. It's his favorite place because his sister works there."

"Thanks, Rosalinda," I said, my heart racing at the prospect of finally getting our hands on Pedro. "You're a lifesaver."

"Be careful, Cam," she warned, her dark eyes filled with concern. "He has men with him."

"Yeah, I know. He always does," I said, a grim smile tugging at the corners of my mouth. "We'll be ready for him."

Jack and I quickly left Rosalinda's and headed straight for Loncheria El Amigo Willy's. The streets were growing darker, the atmosphere tense, as if anticipating a storm. We entered the small eatery, the smell of fried fish and spices filling the air.

"Excuse me," I approached a young woman behind the counter. "We're looking for Pedro. Is he still here?"

"Pedro?" She frowned, her dark eyes clouding with concern. "No, he left already. Are you friends of his?"

"Something like that," I said. "Listen, we need to find him. It's important."

"Pedro..." She sighed, her expression conflicted. "My brother is heading down a dangerous path, and I don't approve of his lifestyle. But I can't tell you where he is."

"We need your help," Jack said.

She looked sadly at us. "He is a bad man," she said, turned and walked away.

Another young woman came to us after his sister was out of sight.

"I heard him talking on the phone earlier, mentioning a house in Moctezuma. It's five miles away on El Cuyo Road. But please, be careful."

"Thank you," I said.

As Jack and I hurried toward the docks, I knew that every second counted. Pedro had Casey, and there was no telling what he would do to him.

We managed to rent a Jeep and took off south on El Cuyo Road.

Chapter 21

The humid air clung to Diane's skin as she sat on her porch in Key West, watching the sun dip below the horizon. She sipped her iced tea, the condensation dripping onto her lap, and her phone buzzed beside her. The screen lit up with Kailey's name, and Diane hesitated for a moment before answering.

"Hi, Diane," Kailey said.

"Kailey," Diane replied, trying to keep her tone steady. "How are you?"

"Fine," Kailey said curtly. Her voice carried an edge that suggested she was anything but fine. "Diane, where's Cam?"

Diane swallowed hard. She didn't want to tell Kailey that Cam was in trouble again - not when Kailey had been away on assignment for a US hit squad called Justice. An efficient assassin, Kailey worked alongside Malinda, taking out enemies of the state with ruthless precision. Diane knew that if Kailey found out about Cam's latest predicament, she'd drop everything and come running.

"Cam?" Diane feigned surprise. "Oh, he's on vacation in El Cuyo."

"El Cuyo?" Kailey's tone softened ever so slightly. "I see."

"I tried to call him, but I didn't get an answer. Is everything okay?"

"As far as I know, it is, but you know how Cam is," she said, making a joke of it.

"True," Kailey admitted with a hint of a smile in her voice. "I'll be back in Key West in a week. Maybe I should go to El Cuyo and surprise him."

She knew that Kailey's unexpected arrival could jeopardize whatever plan Cam had set in motion, not to mention the danger it would bring to both of them. But how could she dissuade Kailey without arousing suspicion?

"Actually," Diane began, trying to sound casual, "Jack is with Cam on this trip. They've been looking forward to some guy time, you know? Just let them have their fun—it's not often they get a chance to unwind together."

"Jack?" Kailey's voice was more relaxed. "So, we both lost our boyfriends. Alright, Diane. I suppose you're right. I'll wait for Cam in Key West."

"Good," Diane said with a sigh of relief. "It'll be nice to have you back, Kailey. We can catch up then."

"Sounds like a plan," Kailey agreed, her tone still guarded.

"If Cam gets into any kind of trouble, like he always seems to do, just call me. Don't hesitate, okay?"

"Of course, Kailey," Diane promised. "I'll keep an eye on things from here."

"Thanks, Diane. I trust you." With that, Kailey ended the call, leaving Diane with a heavy burden on her shoulders.

As she hung up, Diane couldn't help but think about the situation unfolding in El Cuyo. She knew that Jack and Cam were in danger, and a part of her desperately wanted to call Malinda and tell her everything. But she had made a promise to Jack—she wouldn't involve Malinda, at least not yet. If she knew her brother was in trouble, she would be disappointed in Cam.

Diane paced back and forth in her living room, her thoughts a whirlwind of worry and concern. She glanced at the phone. The temptation to call Malinda was almost unbearable, but she knew she had to hold onto that last shred of hope that Cam could handle this on his own.

"Cam, you better know what you're doing," she whispered to herself. "Because if worse comes to worse, I won't hesitate to break that promise."

Every moment that passed felt like an eternity, and all she could do was wait, listen, and hope for the best.

• • • •

THE JEEP'S ENGINE ROARED as I gripped the wheel. Jack sat beside me, his eyes scanning every corner of the small town of Moctezuma. He looked tense. We both had good reason to be.

"Keep an eye out for anything suspicious," I muttered, my voice barely audible over the sound of the engine.

"Like we haven't been doing that already," Jack replied.

"Really, sarcasm?"

"Turn left here," Jack suggested, pointing toward a seemingly innocuous street.

As we turned the corner, a house caught my attention. It stood apart from the others; It was lit up, and several rough-looking characters stood on the front porch drinking beer.

"Pull over," Jack whispered. "This could be it."

"Are you sure?"

"Can't hurt to check," Jack replied as I parked the Jeep a block away under the darkness of a palm tree. We couldn't afford to leave any stone unturned.

"Be careful," I warned as we circled the house to approach it from behind.

"I don't like it," Jack confessed, his voice a whisper. "What if we're walking into a trap?"

"Then we'll deal with it," I said. "We're not leaving without Casey."

"Damn right," Jack agreed, his jaw set in determination.

"Be ready for anything," my hand resting on the gun at my hip, just in case.

We stopped at the rear of the house next door and watched the house. Voices were coming from inside, but filtered out through the open windows. They were hard to understand in Spanish, but once in a while, I heard English. My guess is that was for Casey's benefit. Then I heard someone call, "Pedro!"

I looked at Jack, "Bingo," I whispered. "This is it."

"We need to wait until some of these guys leave and the others pass out," Jack said.

"Yeah, I agree with ya. We'll leave and come back in a few hours. Our best chance will be in the middle of the night."

Staying low and under the cover of darkness, we made our way back to the Jeep. We drove away from the house and circled the block, pulling back onto El Cuyo. In a few minutes, we were back at the marina.

Walter was lying on the deck and jumped up as we approached. I saw Mario lying on the chaise lounge. He was sound asleep.

"How about a drink?" I asked Jack.

"I think I need one," he said.

As I was fixing the drinks, Mario woke up.

"Mister Cam," he said. "Sorry, I fell asleep."

"That's okay. You don't need to stay awake for Walter. If he needs anything, he won't hesitate to wake you."

Mario looked at his watch. "I better go home. It's a long bicycle ride."

"Really, where do you live?" I asked him.

"Moctezuma," he said.

Chapter 22

I watched as Mario fiddled with the frayed edge of his sleeve, the anxiety in his eyes a clear sign that he didn't want to go back to Moctezuma. I couldn't blame him—the small town was a hotbed of danger and violence. I needed him on my boat tonight, not only to watch Walter, but also to keep him safe.

"Hey, Mario," I said, my voice low and steady. "Why don't you call your father and see if you can stay on my boat tonight?"

"Really?" His face lit up with relief, and I nodded.

"Yeah, I could use your help watching Walter. I have some things to do."

"Gracias, Cam," he mumbled. I handed him my phone, and he dialed his father's number. I could hear the tension in his voice as he spoke to his father, asking for permission to stay on my boat.

"Cam, *mi papá dice que sí*," Mario said, hanging up the phone. "He says I can stay on your boat tonight."

"Great," I replied, clapping him on the shoulder. "Let's get settled in, then."

• • • •

PEDRO STOOD OUTSIDE on the back porch, the humid air sticking to his skin. Silvio stood next to him on his cell phone. He said, "Goodnight," and hung up.

"Señor Pedro," Silvio said, keeping his voice low. "I am free tonight to help."

"Silvio, your son Mario will not be home tonight?" Pedro asked, his tone firm yet cautious.

"Actually, no. He's staying with a friend on his boat tonight," Silvio replied.

"Very good."

• • • •

I STARTED TO FEEL A nagging curiosity about Mario's background. I knew he was off-limits since he was just a kid, but with everything that had been going on, I couldn't help but wonder if there was a connection I was missing. It was a long shot, but I needed to know who I was dealing with. I returned to his cabin.

"Hey, Mario," I whispered, "What's your last name?"

"Zara, señor," he answered, his eyes wide with innocence.

The name struck me like lightning.

"What's your father's name?"

"Silvio," he answered.

"Who is Tito's father?"

"Tito doesn't have any family. They were killed in a shipwreck when he was young. Sometimes, he sleep at our house and other times he sleeps in the dock house."

The thought of that sickened me. He is such a good person.

"Alright, kid, get some sleep," I said, forcing a smile and trying to shove the suspicion out of my mind. But deep down, I knew I couldn't ignore the fact that Mario Zara's father worked for Pedro, one of the men I was investigating. I had heard his name once on *Malinda's Star* and again tonight at the house.

I kept running through scenarios in my head. Was this all just a coincidence? Or was Mario somehow involved in his father's shady dealings?

"Cam?" Mario's voice interrupted my thoughts. "Is everything okay?"

I hesitated, torn between wanting to protect the kid and needing answers. In the end, I decided that honesty was the best policy.

"Listen, Mario," I began, looking him straight in the eyes. "I'm not sure what's going on here, but something doesn't feel right. I need you to promise me that you'll stay safe and keep your eyes open, okay?

If you see anything strange or suspicious, you tell me immediately. Understand?"

"*Claro*, Cam," he nodded solemnly. "I promise."

"Good," I replied, feeling the weight of responsibility bearing down on my shoulders. This wasn't just about solving a case anymore. It was about keeping Mario safe from whatever darkness was lurking in the shadows of El Cuyo. And as he settled in for the night, I couldn't help but wonder if I'd be able to protect him from the storm that was brewing on the horizon.

Walter took his cue and lay down next to Mario. I rubbed his head and turned the light off.

Back on the deck, I told Jack of my suspicions. "Do you think Mario could unknowingly be telling his father what we're doing? Maybe his father asks him what he's been doing all day and what we've been up to."

"That could be," Jack said. "I don't think Mario would tell on us on purpose. But he would be more loyal to his father. On the other hand, he would be disappointed if he knew his father worked for Pedro."

"First things first, we keep an extra close eye on Mario," I replied, my resolve steeling. "We need to make sure he stays safe. And then... we figure out how to save Casey without putting Mario's father in danger.

"Alright, Jack. Let's get ready. We've got work to do," I said.

"Remember the plan, Jack," I said, checking my gun one last time before we disembarked. "We approach Moctezuma quietly and cautiously. We don't want to alert Pedro or his men that we're on our way.

Jack just looked at me like I was stupid for stating the obvious. "Yeah, yeah, I was thinking out loud."

We drove the road back to Moctezuma. This time, we parked along the side of the road before we reached the town. We cut across a field that quickly turned into a jungle. Staying on the edge of the tree line, we made our way to the house again.

As we approached the house, I noticed a faint glow behind one of the windows. "Jack, see that?" I whispered, pointing at the dim light. "That could be where they're holding Casey."

"Let's check it out," he responded, his voice just as low.

I nodded, and together, we crept closer to the building, taking care to avoid making any noise. If Silvio was inside, we had to make sure our approach would not put him in danger.

"Cam," Jack murmured, gripping my arm, "Look." He pointed to a figure standing near the entrance, his back turned to us.

"Damn it, that looks like Silvio," I cursed under my breath. "Alright, change of plans. I'll distract Silvio while you sneak around the side and find Casey. We'll rendezvous back here after you spot him. You should be able to see in the windows."

"What's the plan?"

I thought for a minute while I watched him. Then it hit me. "I'll call him. I have his number from Mario using my phone. I'll tell him Mario is sick."

"I guess it's worth a try," Jack said.

The stakes had never been higher, but one thing was certain—we wouldn't back down until we'd done everything in our power to make things right.

<h1>Chapter 23</h1>

The moon was shining bright, casting an eerie glow on the palm trees as they swayed in the gentle sea breeze. Kailey sat on the porch of her beachfront bungalow in Montego Bay, Jamaica, a sense of unease washing over her like the waves crashing against the shore. She couldn't shake the feeling that something was wrong with Cam.

"Diane sounded strange when I talked to her," she muttered to herself, recalling their conversation. It had been brief and tense, not at all like their usual banter. Kailey's instincts told her that Cam was in some sort of trouble, but she couldn't quite put her finger on it.

"Malinda might know something," she thought, picking up her phone and dialing her friend's number. Malinda answered after the second ring, her voice filled with concern.

"Kailey, I was just about to call you. I've been worried about Cam."

"Me too," Kailey replied, her voice wavering slightly. "Diane sounded off when I spoke to her earlier. I think something's going on."

"I talked to Cam earlier. He didn't sound like himself. He said he was lonely."

"Lonely? He has Jack with him, according to Diane."

"When I talked to him, he was alone with Walter."

"Something has happened. He wouldn't call Jack down there if he didn't need help," Kailey said.

"You call Diane back and get the whole story. I'll follow up on some calls I made."

"Will do, but I think she's protecting him."

"Cam's a tough guy, but I can't shake the feeling that he's in danger," Malinda admitted. "I've already spoken to a few people who might help us."

"Thank goodness," Kailey sighed, relieved that someone else shared her concerns. "We need to find out what's going on and make sure he's okay."

"Agreed," Malinda replied firmly. "I'll keep digging and let you know if I find anything."

"Thanks, Malinda. I'll do the same."

As Kailey hung up the phone, her mind raced with thoughts of Cam. He was a strong-willed man who didn't scare easily, but something about this situation made her blood run cold. Determined to uncover the truth and ensure Cam's safety, Kailey resolved to do whatever it took to help him.

"Cam," she whispered into the night, "I'll find you. I promise."

Malinda hung up the phone and immediately began making calls. She needed to send someone to check on Cam without him realizing it, and she knew just the person for the job. A skilled investigator with a knack for blending into the background, he could keep an eye on Cam and report back any suspicious activity.

"Vinicio," Malinda said once her contact answered the call, "It's Brittany, I need you to do me a favor. I have reason to believe that my friend, Cam Derringer, might be in trouble. Can you discreetly follow him and let me know if you see anything out of the ordinary?"

"Of course," Vinicio replied without hesitation. "Consider it done. Is he here in Mexico?"

"El Cuyo," she said.

"Anything for you, Brittany," Vinicio said, using the name he and everyone knows her by in the Caribbean.

"Thank you, Vinicio. Please be careful. I'll send his picture to your phone."

"Don't worry," he assured her before hanging up.

. . . .

I HAD BEEN CONTEMPLATING my next move from the shadows of the dense foliage surrounding the house where I believed Casey was being held. Although I didn't want to put Silvio in harm's way, I couldn't risk losing any more time.

Taking a deep breath, I dialed Silvio's number and disguised my voice as best I could.

"Silvio," I said urgently when the call connected, "you need to get to the marina right away. Mario is sick. He's asking for you."

"Who is this? How did you get this number?" Silvio demanded, suspicion lacing his words.

"Never mind who I am," I insisted, trying to maintain the ruse. "Your son needs you. Go to the marina, now."

Without waiting for a response, I ended the call and watched as Silvio reluctantly left his post on the back porch of the house, clearly torn between duty and family.

With Silvio gone, I wasted no time in signaling to Jack, who had been hiding in the trees nearby. Together, we approached the house cautiously, adrenaline pumping through our veins.

"Let's find Casey," I whispered to Jack. "And put an end to this nightmare once and for all."

"Stay low and keep quiet," I instructed Jack, my voice barely audible. "We don't know who else is inside."

Jack nodded, his expression tense as he followed closely behind me.

Reaching the back door, I carefully tested the handle, holding my breath as it turned silently in my grip. We slipped inside, the darkness of the house enveloping us like a shroud.

As we moved through the rooms, a chilling sense of dread began to creep over me. Every creak of the floorboards seemed to echo like a gunshot, making me flinch involuntarily.

I could hear snoring coming from the main room of the house. It sounded like two or more men were sleeping in there. I held my finger in front of my lips, warning Jack to be quiet. I knew he didn't need the warning, but it was instinct.

"Cam," Jack murmured, gesturing toward a closed door at the end of the hallway. "Should we check in there?"

Nodding, we approached the door.

"You ready?" I asked Jack. He nodded as I eased open the door and stepped into the unknown.

Chapter 24

The door creaked open, revealing a dimly lit room. The smell of sweat and alcohol hit me like a punch to the gut. Jack and I stepped inside, our eyes adjusting to the darkness. A naked man and woman lay sprawled across the bed, their limbs tangled in a mess of sheets. They were out cold, the steady rise and fall of their chests the only sign that they were still alive.

"Shit," Jack whispered under his breath, his eyes flicking between the unconscious pair and me. Our presence was an unwelcome intrusion on whatever had transpired between them, and it was clear we needed to leave––now.

"Let's go," I said quietly, backing out of the room with Jack following close behind. We closed the door gently, leaving the couple to their dreams or nightmares, whichever held them captive.

We made our way outside, the humid air wrapping around us like a suffocating embrace. Sweat trickled down my spine as we moved toward the tree line. Jack wiped his brow with the back of his hand, his eyes searching my face for answers.

"Where the hell is Casey?" he asked, frustration lacing his voice. "Pedro must have moved him."

I shook my head, trying to put the pieces together. "I don't know, but we can't give up." If Pedro thought he could hide Casey from us, he was sorely mistaken.

"Cam, this is getting dangerous," Jack said.

"Then we'll deal with it," I replied, clenching my fists. "Casey's life is on the line, and I won't stand by while Pedro plays his twisted games."

Jack nodded, his jaw set. "Alright, let's keep looking."

Our resolve steeled, we headed back into the fray, ready to face whatever challenges awaited us in our quest to save Casey. The tropical paradise around us now seemed like a sinister labyrinth, but there was no turning back.

The humid air clung to my skin as Jack and I approached the marina, my eyes scanning the area for Silvio. Sweat trickled down my back, but it wasn't just from the oppressive heat—time was running out, and we needed answers.

"Cam, there he is," Jack whispered, pointing to a figure pacing on the dock, his shoulders tense and his gaze darting around.

"Stay here," I instructed Jack, my voice low and controlled. I moved quickly, my footsteps echoing on the weathered planks beneath me. When Silvio finally noticed me, panic flickered across his face, and he bolted.

"Silvio, wait!" I shouted, sprinting after him. My muscles burned, but I managed to catch up, grabbing his arm firmly. "We're not here to hurt you."

"Let me go!" Silvio hissed, fear radiating off him like waves of heat. But I didn't let up my grip.

"Come with me to my boat," I ordered, my tone unwavering. "You'll see Mario's okay." His eyes widened, but he reluctantly nodded, allowing me to lead him toward the yacht.

"Look," I said, pointing to Mario inside the cabin. Silvio's expression softened with relief, but I knew I couldn't waste any more time. "It was me who called you and told you Mario was sick. I wanted to get you away from the house so you wouldn't be harmed."

"Why... why would you do that?" Silvio asked hesitantly, his eyes flicking between Mario and me.

"Because I need your help," I replied. "Pedro's taken Casey, and we have no idea where he is. We need to find him before it's too late."

"Casey?" Silvio swallowed hard, his face paling. "I don't know where he is, Cam. I swear."

"Think, Silvio," I pressed. "Anything you might have seen or heard could be the key to finding him."

As Silvio's eyes searched mine, I could see the gears turning in his head, trying to recall any scrap of information that could lead us to

Casey. The seconds ticked by like hours, each one weighing heavier than the last.

"Please, Silvio. We're running out of time. Did you see anything? Hear anything at all about where Pedro might have taken Casey?"

He hesitated, his gaze shifting. Finally, he spoke, the words tumbling out of him like a dam breaking. "Pedro and two men took him away in a truck. They didn't say where they were going."

"Damn it!" I cursed under my breath, slamming my fist against the railing of the yacht. The lead we had was tenuous, but it was something. I couldn't afford to lose hope now.

"Silvio," I said, forcing myself to stay calm, "I know you don't like working for Pedro. I can see it in your eyes. Help us find Casey, and I promise I'll do everything in my power to keep you and Mario safe."

He looked at me, uncertainty etched across his face. But as his eyes met mine, I saw something else flicker in their depths—a spark of defiance, an ember of rebellion.

"Alright," Silvio said quietly. "I'll help you."

"Thank you," I said.

"Cam," Jack said, his voice tight with worry, "we need to move quickly. Who knows what Pedro has planned for Casey?"

"I know, Jack, but we have to get some sleep or we won't be on our game tomorrow."

"Yeah, you're right," Jack said.

"I'll go back to the house," Silvio said, his voice stronger now. He was determined to prove to Mario he was a good man. "If I hear anything, I'll call you."

"Okay, that would be a great help," I agreed.

Silvio checked on Mario one more time, then left. Jack and I both hit our racks, our muscles were spent, and our wits were on end.

As I lay there, trying to calm my racing thoughts, I couldn't shake the feeling that something wasn't right. We were so close to getting

Casey back, but at what cost? The treasure was still out there, and I knew that Casey and Luke wouldn't just let it go.

I tried to push the thoughts aside and focus on getting some rest, but it was no use. My mind was too wired, too focused on the mission at hand.

Suddenly, there was a knock at the door. I jumped, my hand instinctively going for my weapon.

"Who is it?" I called out, my voice hoarse.

"It's me, Silvio," came the muffled reply.

I let out a sigh of relief and got up to let him in. Silvio looked tired but determined, his eyes scanning the room for any signs of trouble.

"Why are you back already?" I asked him.

"The house," he whispered. "Everyone is dead."

Chapter 25

The morning was late as I stepped off the boat onto the rickety wooden dock. My mission for today--talk to Rosalinda. She always seemed to know what went on in El Cuyo, and maybe she could tell me where Casey and Pedro had gone. Jack stayed behind, watching over things while I was away.

"Cam!" Tito called out from his beachside bar, waving a handkerchief in the air. "You need a soft drink?"

"Maybe later, Tito," I said, squinting against the sunlight reflecting off the water. "I got some business in town."

"Business? In paradise?" he chuckled. "You never can escape it, amigo."

"Unfortunately, not this time," I replied, adjusting my hat to shade my eyes better. Tito sounded so wise for a kid.

The streets were bustling with activity as people went about their daily routines. The scent of fresh seafood filled the air as fishermen returned from their early morning catch. Sweat trickled down my back, but I kept my focus on making my way to Rosalinda's place.

"Cam Derringer?" A voice stopped me in my tracks. A woman approached me, her dark hair cascading over her shoulders. I recognized her as Maria, one of Rosalinda's friends.

"Maria, right?" I asked, trying to sound casual.

"Si, that's me." She looked around nervously. "Rosalinda sent me to find you. She has important information."

"About Casey and Pedro?"

"Come with me," she whispered, leading me through a maze of narrow alleys.

We arrived at a small house with a red door. Maria knocked twice, and it creaked open. Rosalinda peeked out, her eyes wide with fear.

"Cam," she breathed, pulling me inside. "I don't have much time, but I know where Casey and Pedro are."

"Where are they?" I asked, my voice tense.

"Here," she said. "They stayed here at my house last night. This morning they go to Casa De Mar. It is on the east side of town. It once was a grand house, but now not so much. He said he wanted to be close so he could get the treasure.

"Thank you, Rosalinda." My pulse quickened as I prepared to leave. "I'm going to find them."

She gave me directions to the house, then said, "But wait. Pedro said you are in jail. He said he doesn't have to worry about you anymore."

"That's crazy. I'm not in jail."

"Yes, I can see."

"Thanks for your help," I said.

"Be safe," she whispered, tears in her eyes.

As I retraced my steps back to the boat, my thoughts raced faster than my footsteps. Moctezuma. How and when did everyone get killed there? We were just there four hours ago.

"Jack!" I called as I boarded the yacht. "We need to head to Casa De Mar. Rosalinda told me Casey and Pedro are there!"

But there was no response. I scanned the boat, but it was eerily silent. Where had he gone? A growing sense of dread washed over me as I realized something was wrong. That's when Tito approached me with a grim expression on his young face.

"Cam," he said, hesitating for a moment. "The police were here while you were gone. They arrested Jack, thinking he was you."

"They thought he was me?"

"Yes, they say you murdered men last night."

So that was it. Pedro set me up, and the police got the wrong guy. I guess Jack let them believe he was me.

My mind raced, trying to process the information. The police had taken Jack away, and now Pedro was holding Casey at some old house on the east side of town. Time was running out, and I needed to act fast if I wanted to save them and clear my name.

"Thanks, Tito," I said, clapping him on the shoulder. "I appreciate it."

What had happened in Moctezuma? How did we get caught up in this mess? And how was I going to find Casey and Pedro before it was too late?

I knew one thing for certain: I wasn't going to let anyone else get hurt. With determination fueling me, I set out across town for Casa De Mar, ready to confront whatever awaited me there.

"Focus," I muttered to myself, "you need to find Casey and get Jack out of this mess." My steps picked up pace, fueled by the urgency of the situation.

The town seemed eerily quiet, as if it knew something dark was brewing beneath its idyllic surface. I couldn't shake the feeling that eyes were watching me from every corner, assessing my every move.

· · · ·

THE SUN WAS A RELENTLESS fireball in the sky as Vinicio Ferraz's car kicked up dust along the dirt road leading into El Cuyo. Sweat beaded on his forehead, and he wiped it away with the back of his hand, cursing under his breath. Malinda had sent him to check on Cam, but so far, he'd found nothing but heat.

"Where the hell are you, Cam?" Vinicio muttered, gripping the steering wheel tighter. His knuckles turned white from the pressure, and the tension in the air was palpable.

The salty smell of the ocean grew stronger as he pulled up to the docks, the water shimmering like a gemstone beneath the merciless sun. He spotted *The Same Old Song*, Cam's boat, and parked his car nearby, scanning the area for any sign of life. But there was no one.

"Cam? Jack?" Vinicio called out, stepping onto the swaying dock. The only response was the cawing of seagulls overhead. It felt as if the whole town held its breath, waiting for something to happen.

"Over here!" Tito's voice called out from the deck of Cam's yacht. Vinicio breathed a sigh of relief and hurried over to join him.

"Where's Cam? What's going on?" Vinicio asked, his voice strained with concern.

"Are you his friend?" Tito asked.

"Yes, I was sent here to find him by his friend."

Tito's face was grim, and he told Vinicio everything—how the police arrested Jack thinking he was Cam, the trouble with Casey, *Malinda's Star* hiding out in the water with treasure aboard, and that Luke was in the hospital.

"Damn it..." Vinicio muttered, running a hand through his hair. This was worse than he'd imagined. "We need to find Cam and get this sorted out."

"Cam went to find Pedro. He wants to get Casey back and free Jack."

"Good, that's a start." Vinicio's heart raced, his mind working overtime to piece together a plan. "I'll go talk to Luke in the hospital, see if he has any more information about Pedro. You stay here, keep an eye on the boat, and wait for Cam. We'll figure this out. Tell him I'm a friend of Brittany's."

"Be careful, Vinicio," Tito warned. "There are bad men."

Vinicio thought Tito sounded awfully tough for sixty pounds.

"Trust me, I know." Vinicio's eyes darkened with determination. There wasn't time to waste. He needed to find answers, and fast.

As he left the dock, Vinicio dreaded the call he must make to Brittany now. She was going to be furious at Cam for getting into trouble again. He wondered if Brittany knew who Casey and Luke were.

"Cam, I hope you're finding what you need," Vinicio whispered to himself, stepping into the car and starting the engine. The stakes had never been higher, and it was up to him to make sure they survived.

Chapter 26

The heat of the tropical sun, casting shadows that danced with the sway of palm trees. Vinicio wiped beads of sweat from his brow as he dialed Malinda's number.

"Brittany, it's Vinicio," he said, urgency lacing his voice. "Cam and Jack are in deep trouble. The police have got Jack, thinking he's Cam, and they're holding him for murder."

A pause, then Brittany's steady voice came through. "What do you mean? How did this happen?"

"Listen, I don't have all the details, but there's a man named Casey involved. He's got a boat called the *Malinda's Star.*" Vinicio glanced around nervously as if afraid someone might be listening.

"Casey?" Brittany murmured, her tone betraying a hint of recognition. "Okay, thanks for letting me know, Vinicio. I'll take care of it. You keep an eye on them until I get there."

As the call disconnected, Vinicio's hands trembled slightly. He hoped he had done the right thing, but only time would tell.

. . . .

BRITTANY'S HEART RACED as she processed the information. Casey—her brother who believed she was dead, and Cam—the man she has always loved. The two of them were connected, and she had to find out how.

"Casey, what have you gotten yourself into?" she whispered under her breath, memories of their past life together flooding her mind. She shook her head, forcing herself to focus on the present.

Brittany called Kailey. As the phone rang, Brittany envisioned the woman's deadly skills put to use as an assassin, just like her own.

"Kailey, it's Brittany," she said when the call connected. "We've got a problem. Cam and my brother Casey are mixed up in something dangerous, and Jack's been arrested in Cam's place for murder"

"Damn," Kailey muttered, her voice as cold as ice. "What do we do?"

Brittany replied, her voice resolute. "We're going to El Cuyo to sort this mess out."

As Brittany stared at her phone, she couldn't help but feel a sense of foreboding. Whatever awaited them in El Cuyo, it wouldn't be easy. But she knew one thing for certain: she would fight tooth and nail to protect those she loved.

· · · ·

"UNDERSTOOD," KAILEY responded, and with that, she glanced at the man who was tied to the chair in her bungalow.

Kailey hung up and stood. "My plans are changed," she said to the bound man. "Are you going to tell me who has the documents for the nuclear missile control?"

The man stared into Kailey's eyes with a determined will. "Never," he said.

Kailey picked up the silenced pistol on the dresser and shot the man in the forehead.

· · · ·

I APPROACHED THE WORN and abandoned-looking house. It seemed out of place in its tropical surroundings—a relic from a bygone era.

As I neared the house, I spotted Pedro stepping out onto the porch. I could see the sweat glistening on his forehead as he scanned the area with a sense of unease.

I ducked behind a cluster of overgrown bushes, their thorns pricking at my skin. I held my breath, watching intently as Pedro paced back and forth on the porch.

Finally, after what felt like an eternity, Pedro turned and stepped back inside the house.

I crept closer to the house, ready to face whatever challenges awaited me within its walls.

I reached the back door and paused for a moment, listening intently for any signs of movement inside. Satisfied that the coast was clear, I carefully pushed the door open and slipped inside, my gun at the ready.

The house was darker than I expected, the sunlight barely penetrating the dusty windows. It felt like stepping into another time, where secrets lay hidden beneath layers of decay. My footsteps seemed to echo through the silence, each creaking floorboard setting my nerves on edge.

As I made my way through the dimly lit rooms, I caught the faint scent of food wafting through the air. Following my nose, I found myself in the kitchen, where Pedro stood with his back to me, fixing lunch. The savory aroma almost made me forget why I was there.

"Put your hands in the air," I ordered in a low, steady voice, my gun aimed squarely at Pedro's back.

He froze, his body tensing as he slowly raised his hands above his head. "What do you want?" he demanded, fear evident in his voice.

"Take me to Casey," I responded firmly, maintaining my aim. Pedro hesitated for a moment, glancing nervously around the kitchen before nodding in resignation.

"Alright, come with me," he said, leading me through the dark, narrow halls of the house. Each step we took only heightened the suspense, the weight of what was happening settling heavily on me.

"Where is he?" I asked, my impatience growing by the second.

"Upstairs," Pedro replied, his voice shaking. "In one of the bedrooms."

We reached the top of the staircase, and Pedro led me down another dimly lit hallway. The thick air hung heavy with the scent of mildew and neglect.

"Here," Pedro whispered, stopping in front of a worn, wooden door. I pushed it open. I saw Casey, bound and gagged, slumped against the wall. Relief washed over me as I saw he was still alive, though it was clear he had been through hell.

"Untie him," I hissed at Pedro, keeping my gun trained on him. He reluctantly obeyed, his hands trembling as he fumbled with the knots. As soon as Casey was free, I wasted no time securing Pedro to the bed, ensuring he wouldn't be following us anytime soon.

"Cam," Casey croaked, his voice weak but filled with gratitude. "How did you find me?"

"Later," I replied. "Right now, we need to get Jack out of police custody."

"Jack?" Casey's brow furrowed in confusion. "What happened?"

I explained the situation quickly, knowing that time was of the essence. Casey's eyes widened in disbelief, but he nodded grimly, understanding the gravity of our predicament.

Pedro laughed. "They were supposed to arrest you," he said.

"Yeah, but they didn't, and I'm going to make sure they know it was you who murdered those men."

"I don't know what you're talking about," he mused.

"Let's go," I said to Casey, determination hardening my features.

We made our way cautiously back through the house. As we slipped out the back door, I couldn't help but think about the irony of our situation—the police holding the wrong man while the one they were after was about to walk right up to their doorstep.

"Listen," I told Casey as we neared the police station. "We need to make a plan. If they see me, they'll know they have the wrong man and arrest me on the spot. Let's go back to the boat first."

"Where's Luke?" he asked.

"In the hospital, but he's going to be okay."

"I wanna go see him."

"Alright, I'll meet you at my boat in an hour. Be careful. I don't think it'll be long before Pedro is set free by one of his goons."

"I don't think any of them know where he is. I heard him on the phone before we left. He didn't tell anyone where we were going."

"Good. I'll call the police and tell them where Pedro is and that he was the one who killed those guys."

"There's no proof. I didn't see him do it."

"Cam Derringer?" a voice came from behind me.

I turned to see a Mexican man standing a few feet away. I prepared myself for another fight. He was tall and slim with well-defined muscles. He wore tan slacks and a white shirt. His Panama hat was pulled down in front, shading his eyes.

"Who wants to know?" I asked cautiously.

"Vinicio Ferraz. Brittany sent me."

I glanced quickly at Casey who was watching the man.

"Who's Brittany?" Casey asked.

"An old friend with connections," I said quickly. "You go to the hospital, and I'll handle this."

"Got it," he replied, a steely resolve in his voice. I watched as he walked away from me, toward the hospital, my heart pounding. This was it—the moment where everything could either fall into place or come crashing down around us.

"Let's go to my boat to talk," I said after Casey was gone. "Don't mention Brittany in front of Casey again."

We started our walk to the boat.

"That was Casey?" he asked.

"Yeah."

"Good. Brittany seemed to be upset when I told her he was in trouble."

"She knows about him?"

"Yes, it was my job to fill her in. I will never lie to her."

"Yeah, I guess not. It wouldn't be wise."

"But I think maybe you already have," Vinicio said.

"It was for her own good."

I couldn't shake the feeling that we were walking a fine line between salvation and disaster. And only time would tell which side we'd ultimately end up on.

Chapter 27

I sat on my boat with Vinicio. The ice in my Wild Turkey clinked gently against the glass, Walter resting his head on my feet. It was one of those evenings where you could almost forget about the trouble brewing around you.

I decided I couldn't wait any longer. I called the police and was put through to Sargent Sal Pesina.

"How can I help you?" he asked in a heavy Spanish accent.

"This Cam Derringer," I said, waiting for a reaction.

After a slight hesitation, he said, "And?"

"Doesn't that name sound familiar to you?"

"Should it?"

"Don't you have me locked up in your jail?"

"Just a minute, sir," he said and held his hand over the phone. I could hear him talking to someone in Spanish.

He came back to the phone, "Mister Derringer," he said, "we have no one locked in our jail. Maybe you should check with the Cancun police department. We have only one cell here, and it is empty."

"Did you arrest a man at the docks today for murder?"

Another slight hesitation. "No, sir. We did not."

"Do you have the number for the Cancun Police Department?" I asked.

He gave me the number, and I wrote it down. I thanked him and hung up.

"Jack's not at the police station here," I told Vinicio.

"Where the hell is he then?"

"I don't know, but I know who does."

"I'm going to go see Pedro again."

"Cam," Vinicio said, taking a sip from his own drink, "you've got to be careful with this Pedro guy."

"Trust me, Vinicio, I know," I replied, stroking Walter's golden fur.

That's when I saw her. Rosalinda walked toward us along the dock, her footsteps echoing softly. She surprised me—I hadn't expected her to show up here.

"Cam, are you okay?" she asked, genuine concern in her eyes.

"Rosalinda, what are you doing here?" I questioned, startled by her sudden appearance.

"I wanted to see if you were alright," she explained, shifting her weight nervously from one leg to another. "And I wanted to help in finding Pedro and proving him guilty."

"Help? How?" I inquired, skeptical but intrigued.

"Look, I know Pedro," she began, hesitating slightly. "I know how he thinks, and I know his weaknesses. I want to make sure he gets what he deserves."

"Alright," I said cautiously, trying to gauge her intentions. "But why do you want to help me?"

"Because," she started, then paused, looking down at the wooden planks beneath her feet, "because I can't stand to see what he's done to this town. And to you."

"Okay," I agreed reluctantly, feeling a strange mix of gratitude and apprehension. "We'll figure this out together."

"Thank you, Cam," she said, relief washing over her face. "I won't let you down."

"I already know where Pedro is, though. I was just about to go see him."

Her eyes widened. "Where is he?"

"I have him tied up in that old house you told me about."

She sat down in one of my chairs.

"Here," I offered, fixing her a drink. "You look like you could use this."

"Thanks," she smiled, taking the glass from my hand. Her smile faltered for just a moment as she added, "I know this is going to be dangerous, Cam. But I'm ready."

"Let's just hope it doesn't come to that," I replied, feeling the weight of responsibility settle on my shoulders. The last thing I wanted was to put her in harm's way.

"Yes," she said nervously.

"Pedro claims you're his girl," I said, narrowing my eyes at Rosalinda. "Is that true?"

"According to him, maybe," she scoffed, rolling her eyes. "But I've never felt anything for him. In fact, I'd be your girl if you could get rid of Pedro from this town."

"Look, Rosalinda," I said, trying to keep my tone light despite the seriousness of the situation, "I might have a few women in my life, but that doesn't mean I'm collecting them like trophies. I'll help you with Pedro, but not because I want something in return."

"Okay," she replied hesitantly, clearly taken aback by my answer. "But just know that I'm here to help, too. I don't want him causing any more trouble."

"Deal," I agreed, nodding my head. "Now I have to go. I need to find out where Jack is."

"Jack?" she asked. "Isn't he in jail?"

"No, not here anyway."

"Cam, are you sure about this?" Vinicio asked, a hint of concern lacing his voice.

"Vinicio, I've dealt with worse. Besides, we can't let Pedro continue what he's doing. It's time someone put an end to it."

"I'll go with you to talk to him then," he said, standing. His imposing figure could be a plus if there were trouble.

"Alright," Vinicio sighed. "Let's do this."

I looked at Rosalinda, trying to gauge her thoughts. She seemed determined, yet there was a vulnerability behind her eyes that made me want to protect her. But I had to remind myself that she wasn't some damsel in distress—she was strong, and she'd made it clear she wanted to stand up against Pedro.

"Are you ready for this?" I asked her softly, searching her gaze.

"More than anything," she whispered back, her voice trembling just slightly.

I glanced down at Walter, who had taken quite a liking to Rosalinda. He leaned against her legs, wagging his tail happily as she scratched behind his ears. Despite the tense atmosphere surrounding our conversation, it seemed that my trusty golden retriever had found an unlikely friend in this mysterious woman.

"Cam," Rosalinda said, breaking through my thoughts. "You really think we can do it? Take him down, I mean."

There it was again, that rare glimpse of uncertainty in her eyes. I took a deep breath, weighing my words carefully.

"Rosalinda," I began solemnly, "I can't promise it'll be easy or without risk. But I swear to you, I will do everything in my power to make sure Pedro doesn't hurt anyone else. And I have a feeling that once he realizes he's not as untouchable as he thinks, the people of this town will stand up to him too."

Her smile returned, albeit with a touch of sadness. "I hope you're right, Cam," she said softly. "For all our sakes."

"Me too," I replied, sipping my drink and letting the burn of the whiskey fire up my determination. It was time to take action. For El Cuyo. For Rosalinda. And for everyone who'd ever been wronged by Pedro and his thugs.

The boat gently rocked beneath us, lulling us into a false sense of security. I could hear the distant laughter of people on the beach, their joy only heightening the contrast between our worlds.

"Cam," Rosalinda said, breaking the silence. "If we succeed...what happens next?"

I sighed, hesitant to make promises I wasn't sure I could keep. "We'll cross that bridge when we get there, Rosalinda."

Chapter 28

The sun had dipped beneath the horizon, leaving only a faint orange glow on the edge of the sea. The salty air clung to my skin as Vinicio and I approached the abandoned house.

"Ready?" Vinicio murmured, his dark eyes scanning the area for any sign of danger.

"Let's do it," I replied.

We eased our way inside, silently stepping over shattered glass and rotting debris. The house smelled of damp mold and salt, a scent that seemed to crawl into my lungs, making it harder to breathe with each step.

Pedro was still there, tied to the bed just as we had left him. His face lit up when he saw me, a wicked grin spreading across his lips.

"Ah, Cam, I knew you'd be back," he chuckled, his laughter sending chills down my spine. "I figured you'd realize soon enough that Jack wasn't where you thought he was."

I clenched my fists. How could he know about Jack? What had they done with him?

"Where is he?" I demanded, taking a menacing step towards Pedro. "Talk now, or I swear I'll make you wish you had."

"Easy, amigo," Pedro sneered, his eyes darting over to Vinicio before settling back on me. "You two have no leverage here, so don't go making threats you can't keep."

"Maybe not yet," I growled. "But believe me, Pedro, your time is running out."

"Is that so?" He laughed again, the sound echoing around the rotting room like the cackle of some demonic bird. "Well, you better hurry up then, because I don't think Jack has much time left."

"Enough!" I roared, my patience snapping. "Tell me where he is, or so help me–"

"Or what?" Pedro interrupted, his voice cold and cruel. "You can't do anything to me, Cam. I'm not the one you should be worried about."

Vinicio suddenly chimed in, the irritation evident in his voice. "Pedro, you won't be laughing when Brittany shows up."

"Brittany?" I asked, momentarily surprised. My heart raced as I tried to understand what Vinicio was getting at. "Is Brittany coming here?"

"Surprised?" Vinicio smirked, his gaze never leaving Pedro's face. "You didn't think we'd come here without a plan, did you?"

"Brittany?" Pedro repeated, his bravado waning just a bit. "You mean... her?"

"Of course, who else would I be talking about? And she's not alone. They'll take down your whole gang if you don't tell us where Jack is now," Vinicio warned him.

For the first time since we had entered the room, I saw a flicker of fear in Pedro's eyes. But it wasn't enough, not yet. I needed him to crack, to reveal Jack's whereabouts before it was too late.

The sweat beaded on Pedro's forehead, his eyes darting nervously between Vinicio and me. I could almost smell his fear, like an animal backed into a corner, knowing the hunter had it trapped.

"Untie me," Pedro demanded, his voice shaking ever so slightly. "Give me your phone."

I hesitated, glancing at Vinicio for confirmation. He gave a terse nod, and I tossed my phone onto the bed beside Pedro. His hands fumbled with the device, fingers slippery from perspiration.

* * * *

DEEP IN THE JUNGLE, Jack stumbled forward, his hands bound and two policemen at his side. They had led him away from the jailhouse with one goal in mind: to eliminate him without a trace. Sweat dripped down his brow as he struggled to keep up with their pace, the thick foliage surrounding them closing in like a suffocating vice.

"Keep moving," grunted one of the men, shoving Jack roughly in the back. "We ain't got all day."

Jack's heart raced as he desperately searched for any chance of escape. Though he was no stranger to danger, this situation felt different—more sinister and final. I can't die here, not like this, he thought, gritting his teeth.

"Wait," said the other man suddenly, pulling out a phone as it buzzed in his hand. His brow furrowed as he listened to Pedro's frantic instructions on the other end of the line.

"Boss says we're bringing him back," he announced, lowering the phone and eyeing his partner skeptically. "Unharmed. We have the wrong man."

The first man scowled but reluctantly nodded. "Fine. Let's go."

With a mixture of relief and confusion, Jack allowed himself to be led back in the direction they came from. He couldn't help but wonder what had changed Pedro's mind—and more importantly, who had orchestrated this sudden reprieve.

As they trekked back through the dense undergrowth, Jack knew that Cam was still fighting for him. Little did he know just how close they were to turning the tables on Pedro and his gang.

• • • •

HIS EYES LOCKED ONTO mine, and I saw the dawning realization that he'd underestimated us. He ended the call and threw the phone back at me, anger and resignation etched on his face.

"Your friend will be returned," he muttered, glaring daggers at me. "But this isn't over, Cam. You'll regret crossing us."

"Save your threats," I snapped, grabbing the phone and shoving it into my pocket. "We'll deal with you and your gang once Jack is safe."

A wicked smile twisted Pedro's lips as his gaze flicked between Vinicio and me. "You think you've won? Just remember, Cam, there's always someone stronger, smarter... deadlier than you out there. And when they find you, you'll wish you had never crossed paths with me."

"Save it for Brittany," I whispered, my words a promise as I tied him to the bed again. Whatever consequences awaited me, I knew that saving Jack was worth the risk. And as for Pedro and his gang? They would face justice—one way or the other.

Chapter 29

My mind was fixated on *Malinda's Star* and the treasure it held. Would it still be there? Or had someone else already claimed it?

"Ah, Señor Cam, Rosalinda is still here," Vinicio said as he pointed toward my boat. There she was, lounging on the deck, her dark hair cascading over her shoulders like a waterfall, not quite covering her bare breasts.

"Hey, Rosalinda," I called out, trying not to sound too distracted by the thoughts swirling in my head.

"Cam!" She waved at us with a bright smile that belied the tension I felt building inside me.

As we climbed aboard, I couldn't shake the gnawing feeling that the treasure was slipping through my fingers. Time was running out, and I needed to act. "Vinicio, keep an eye on things here. I need to check something."

"Sure thing," he replied, his eyes darting between Rosalinda and me.

I hopped into the tender and started the motor, heading towards *Malinda's Star*. The waves crashed against the small vessel, but I barely noticed.

I searched the area onboard where they told me they had hidden it. There it was. The treasure. It was still here.

My first instinct was to bring it back up with me, but I hesitated. If word got out about its discovery, chaos would ensue. No, it was better to keep it a secret for now. Taking the heavy duffel in my arms, I swam beneath the ship and buried it deep in the ocean floor, right under *Malinda's Star*.

Once I was satisfied with its hiding place, I kicked my way back up to the surface, gasping for air as I broke through. Climbing into the tender, I glanced back at my boat, where Vinicio and Rosalinda awaited my return. It was done—the treasure was safe, hidden away from prying eyes. But for how long?

As I pulled the tender up alongside my boat, Vinicio looked at me curiously. "You look wet," he observed.

"Moved a few things around," I said with a casual shrug, not wanting to reveal too much. Vinicio's expression remained skeptical, but he didn't press for more information.

Rosalinda, still topless, silently handed me a towel as I stepped back onto the deck, her eyes searching mine for any hint of what had transpired. I offered her a small smile, trying to convey that everything was under control. For now, at least.

"Jack should be here soon," I said, changing the subject. We all positioned ourselves on the deck, eyes scanning the dock for any sign of our friend.

Sure enough, a few minutes later, Jack appeared at the dock. There was something in his stride—an air of confidence mixed with weariness—that marked him as a man who had seen his fair share of trouble.

"Hey, Cam!" Jack called out, waving as he approached us. "Rosalinda. Good to see you both."

"Good to see you too, Jack," I replied, shaking his hand firmly. "Listen, Brittany sent Vinicio here. She's on her way too."

"Brittany?" Jack's eyebrows shot up in surprise. "Now that's going to make things interesting."

We exchanged knowing glances. Brittany had a knack for turning even the calmest of situations into whirlwinds of chaos. But she was also resourceful and cunning—qualities we would likely need in the days to come.

"Interesting" was one word for it. "Trouble" might have been more accurate.

"Cam, you know you'll be in trouble when she gets here," Jack said, chuckling. "She's always having to save your ass."

I couldn't help but grin at the truth of his statement. Brittany had a habit of swooping in just in the nick of time to pull me out of whatever mess I'd managed to get myself into.

"True," I admitted, leaning against the railing. "But it could be worse. Kailey could be coming too."

The mention of Kailey sent a shudder down my spine. If Brittany was a whirlwind, Kailey was a hurricane—fierce, unpredictable, and utterly destructive. The thought of them both descending upon El Cuyo was enough to make me question my sanity.

"Let's just hope we can keep things under control until we figure out our next move," I muttered, more to myself than anyone else. But as I glanced over at Vinicio, Rosalinda, and Jack, I knew that was easier said than done.

"Keep our fingers crossed," Jack agreed, casting a wary glance at the dock.

Not a moment too soon, we spotted a familiar figure walking up the dock. The air seemed to thicken with tension as her confident stride brought her closer. Kailey had arrived, her flowing black hair unmistakable even from a distance.

"Wow, who is that?" Rosalinda asked, her curiosity piqued.

I swallowed hard, trying to steady my nerves. There was no telling what kind of storm Kailey would bring with her, and I couldn't shake the uneasy feeling in the pit of my stomach.

"Kailey," I said simply, not wanting to elaborate on the potential problems her presence could cause. My heart raced as she approached the boat, and I braced myself for whatever chaos might follow.

"Cam! Long time, no see." Kailey's voice rang out as she stepped aboard, her piercing green eyes flashing with amusement.

"Hey, Kailey. What brings you here?" I attempted to sound casual, but the words came out more like a croak.

"Can't a girl just drop by and say hello to her boyfriend?" She smirked, tossing her hair over one shoulder. "Or do you have something to hide?"

"Nothing to hide here," I replied, forcing a laugh. But beneath the surface, my mind raced with questions and concerns. What did Kailey know? How much trouble were we really in?

"Good," she said, her eyes narrowing slightly. "Because I'm here to help, whether you like it or not." She looked at Jack, "Glad to see you're out of jail."

Shit, she knows everything.

As I exchanged a worried glance with Jack, I knew one thing for certain—with both Brittany and Kailey in El Cuyo, there was no escaping the fact that we were neck-deep in trouble. And getting out wouldn't be easy.

I stepped closer to her, and she moved to me at the same time. We embraced and kissed softly. "I missed you," I said.

"I missed you too," she replied. "Why is there a topless woman on your boat?"

"Oh," I said. I turned toward Rosalinda and introduced the two women.

"Nice to meet you," Kailey said.

"And you."

There was an uneasy silence that lasted way too long as the two women stared at each other.

"She's Pedro's girlfriend," I said, feeling my face turning red.

Kailey, still looking at Rosalinda, said, "He's cute when he's flustered, isn't he?"

They both giggled.

"Why is Pedro's girlfriend on your boat, then?" Kailey asked.

"She doesn't really want him to be her boyfriend. It's his idea. She's here to help us," I said.

Kailey looked at Vinicio. "You're looking good," she said and hugged him.

"You two know each other?" I asked. "Of course you do."

Then, removing her top, Kailey sat down and said, "We need a plan."

Chapter 30

I stood on the deck of my yacht, trying to catch a glimpse of Brittany's arrival. The sun was setting, casting an orange glow across the water and painting the sky in warm colors. A gentle breeze rustled through the trees that lined the shore. It was peaceful, but I couldn't shake the uneasiness that lingered.

"Hey, Cam," Kailey said softly, approaching me cautiously as if she didn't want to startle me. "Everything okay?"

"Fine," I replied gruffly, not wanting to let her in on my thoughts just yet. "Any word from Brittany? When's she gonna be here?"

"Shouldn't be long now," she answered, glancing nervously toward the dock. "But we have to make sure Casey doesn't see her."

"Right," I agreed, rubbing my chin thoughtfully. "That would be...awkward. He still thinks she's dead."

We fell silent, both lost in our thoughts. As much as I tried to keep a cool exterior, the suspense gnawed at me.

"Casey should be back soon," I informed Kailey, trying to keep my voice steady. "He went to the hospital to see Luke."

"Luke's okay, right?" she asked, concern etched on her face.

"Seems so. Took a nasty hit, though," I admitted, remembering the sight of Luke's battered body. My fists clenched involuntarily at the memory.

"Good. We need all the help we can get," she murmured, her gaze fixed on the distant shoreline.

As we stood there, waiting, I couldn't help but wonder how everything had gone so wrong. What started as a simple vacation in El Cuyo had turned into a deadly game. And now, with Brittany's return imminent and the stakes higher than ever, I had to wonder if we'd make it out alive.

"I'm surprised there is a hospital here," Kailey said suddenly, breaking the silence.

"It's very small," I replied, offering her a thin smile. "Luckily, it had what we needed for Luke."

"Key West has spoiled us with its conveniences, hasn't it?" she mused, her expression softening slightly.

"Indeed. But don't let El Cuyo's quaint charm fool you," I warned, my voice low and serious. "We have to stay vigilant. There's more going on around here than meets the eye."

Kailey nodded solemnly, her eyes meeting mine. We both understood the gravity of the situation, even if we didn't know exactly what fate had in store for us.

"Cam," she started hesitantly, "what do you think will happen when Brittany gets here?"

I sighed, running a hand through my hair. "Honestly, I don't know. But one thing's for sure: we need to be prepared for anything. This is her kingdom."

"Right," she agreed. "We'll make her step back and take a look. She'll be mad about her brother, and she might be mad at you too."

"Yep, I expect she will. For now, all we could do was wait – wait for Casey and Luke to return, wait for Brittany's arrival, wait for the storm that would inevitably follow."

Just then, I noticed two familiar figures walking up the dock. Casey had returned, supporting Luke, who was moving slowly but seemed to be on the mend. The expression on their faces changed from relief to surprise as they took in the sight of Kailey and Rosalinda standing there, both topless. They clearly hadn't been expecting their company.

"Hey guys," I called out, trying to keep my tone casual despite the tension I felt inside. "Meet Kailey."

"Nice to meet you," Kailey said, extending her hand toward Casey and Luke.

"Uh, yeah, nice to meet you too," Luke replied, his eyes darting between us, searching for an explanation. Casey simply nodded, his face unreadable.

"Good to see you're doing better, Luke," I added, genuine concern in my voice. He had been through a lot, and I wanted him to know we were all in this together.

"Thanks, Cam," he replied, a small smile forming on his lips. "It's been... quite an experience."

"El Cuyo sure has its surprises," Casey said, trying to break the tension in the air. He glanced at Kailey and Rosalinda before settling his gaze on me, eyes narrowing slightly as if asking for an explanation.

"Let's just say we've had an interesting time while you were at the hospital," I said, keeping my voice steady despite the urge to reveal everything that had transpired. It wasn't the right moment, and I needed to protect not just Brittany's secret but also Kailey's true identity.

"Seems like it," Luke chuckled, wincing a bit as he clutched his side. "Glad I didn't miss out on all the fun."

"Luke, maybe you should take it easy for now," Casey suggested, concern etched on his face. "We can catch up later."

"Probably a good idea," Luke agreed, giving us all a weak smile as Casey helped him onto the boat.

As they disappeared below deck, Kailey turned to me, her eyes flashing with urgency. "Cam, we need to keep this under control. If Casey finds out about Brittany, everything will unravel."

I nodded, understanding the gravity of the situation. "Yeah, we'll manage."

She smiled, the tension in her shoulders easing ever so slightly. "Yeah," she replied softly. "Together."

"Right," I said, clapping my hands together to refocus our attention on the present. "Let's make sure we're all on the same page."

"Agreed," Kailey replied, glancing over at Rosalinda.

"First off, Casey and Luke can't know about your true identity or that Brittany is alive.

"Secondly, Kailey, you'll need to play it cool around Casey and Luke. We don't want them getting suspicious about anything," I continued, watching as she processed my words.

"Understood," she said, her eyes reflecting a determination that only grew stronger with each passing moment.

"Lastly," I added, "we need to find the right time to bring Brittany here without alerting anyone else. Timing is crucial if we're going to pull this off."

"Cam, I'm confident we can do this," Kailey reassured me. "I've dealt with far more complicated situations before."

"Good," I sighed.

As we wrapped up our conversation, Casey emerged from below deck, his face flushed from helping Luke settle in.

"Everything okay?" he asked, raising an eyebrow at the serious atmosphere.

"Of course," I replied with a forced grin, slapping him on the back. "Just planning our next move. The adventure never stops, does it?"

Casey laughed, shaking his head. "No, it certainly doesn't."

"By the way," I said, turning my attention back to Kailey. "I have Pedro tied up in a house on the other end of town. His men have probably found and released him by now, but at least we bought ourselves some time."

"Pedro? The drug lord?" Kailey's eyes widened, her expression a mix of surprise and concern. "You really don't shy away from danger, do you?"

"Part of the job."

"Let's go see him now," Kailey suggested, her eyes darkening with determination. "Maybe we can find something useful before his men find him—or us."

"Alright, let's give it a try," I agreed, not wanting to waste any time. As we began to step off the yacht, Kailey's cell phone rang, causing her to pause.

"Hello?" she answered, her voice tense. A moment passed, and her eyes widened in shock as she listened to the person on the other end. "Brittany!" she whispered, glancing nervously around.

"Is everything okay?" I asked.

"Something's wrong," Kailey murmured, her grip on the phone tight enough to whiten her knuckles. "She needs our help. Some gunmen have her pinned down on the road leading here. She's about a mile out."

"Change of plans," I said. "We'll deal with Pedro later. Right now, we need to get to Brittany."

"Agreed," Kailey nodded, her eyes alight with worry and determination. "Lets go."

I grabbed several rifles. Jack picked his gun up, and we all ran to Kailey's car.

"Vinicio, will you stay here and watch these guys?" I asked.

"I can better help you," he said.

"Please, Vinicio," Kailey said.

He relented. "They'll be okay. Get going."

Chapter 31

The screech of tires cut through the humid air as we skidded to a halt, dust and gravel spraying from beneath our wheels. I could see Brittany pinned down behind her car, five armed men closing in on her position. My heart raced, adrenaline pumping through my veins like wildfire.

"Let's blast these bastards!" I shouted, already feeling the weight of my gun in my hand. But Kailey grabbed my arm, stopping me short.

"Wait," she hissed, her eyes sharp and focused. "We need a plan."

"Every second counts, Kailey," I muttered. But she was already moving, popping the trunk of the car open with a swift kick. The metal lid creaked as it swung upwards, revealing its deadly cargo: a sleek, black sniper rifle nestled in a custom foam case.

"Cover me," Kailey ordered, her voice steady as she assembled the weapon. I gritted my teeth and nodded, watching the menacing figures advance on Brittany. Jack took position beside me, his face set in a grim expression.

"Ready?" he asked, his voice low. I nodded, my grip tightening on my weapon.

"Ready."

Kailey moved like a shadow, her lithe body slipping between trees and foliage as she climbed a nearby hill. I held my breath, waiting for her signal.

"Three... two... one..." Her fingers counted down as I watched her. And then the first shot rang out.

"Go, go, go!" I shouted, surging forward with Jack at my side. The gunmen scrambled for cover as Kailey picked them off one by one—a deadly dance of precision and skill. Each shot seemed to echo in my ears, a symphony of violence and chaos.

Damn, she's good, I thought. *But who are these guys? And why the hell do they want Brittany dead?*

As Kailey took down another man, I charged forward, adrenaline pumping through my veins. Jack and I moved as a team, our years of experience together making us an efficient unit. We had each other's backs, and it felt good to have him by my side in the fray.

"Last one," Kailey whispered to herself. "I'm going for his leg."

A shot rang out, and the last man crumpled to the ground, clutching his leg in agony. As I approached, his eyes widened in fear, sweat pouring down his face. Jack held him down while I kneeled beside him, my voice a low growl.

"Talk," I demanded, staring deep into his panicked eyes. "Who are you? Why are you after Brittany?"

"Please," he gasped, pain etched into his features. "I don't know her name. They just told us to kill her! Said she knew too much."

"Who?" I pressed, anger simmering beneath my calm exterior. "Who sent you?"

"Boss... he never shows his face. Just calls the shots. Please, man, that's all I know!"

"Is it Pedro?"

"No, no, Pedro works for him, too."

I looked at Jack, who looked as surprised as me.

Kailey arrived as Brittany walked up to us.

"What's he have to say?" Brittany asked.

"He doesn't know who hired him. Just that they wanted you dead."

"He knows," she said, kneeling down next to him. She put her hand on his wound and squeezed. He yelled out pain. "Stop!"

"Tell me who sent you?" she spat. And squeezed harder.

"Pascual Duran," he cried.

"The politician?" she said, surprised.

The man nodded his head repeatedly.

"Shit," she said and stood.

"Do you know him?" I asked.

"We're working on revitalizing Yucatán together. Evidently, he has other plans for the country."

Brittany looked back down at the man. "Tell him I will be seeing him soon."

Then Brittany looked at me. She didn't have to say what she was thinking. I got the message. "Where's Casey?"

"He's back at my boat. Everything is okay now. You didn't need to come here." But as I said the words, I knew it wasn't true. So did Brittany.

She hugged me and said, "I love you. Now let's get into town and find Pedro. I want to see if he has the same story this guy had."

"What will we do with him?" I asked, looking down at the man who was holding his leg and crying.

"They'll pick him up," she said, pointing at a dust cloud coming our way. "We had better get out of here now."

We ran to our cars and headed to El Cuyo.

The air was heavy with the scent of decay as we approached the abandoned house. Jack, Kailey, Brittany, and I moved cautiously through the overgrown path that led to the crumbling structure.

"Pedro should be here," Jack whispered, his words barely audible above the hum of insects. We were all on edge, unsure of what we would find inside.

"Stay close," I warned them, taking the lead as we entered the dilapidated building. The floorboards creaked beneath our feet, and the shadows seemed to move with a life of their own.

I led them to where we had Pedro tied to a bed. But there was no sign of Pedro. He was gone.

"Damn it!" I muttered under my breath. How had he escaped? And where had he gone?

"Cam, what now?" Brittany asked.

"Plan B," I replied, trying to sound more confident than I felt. "We need to find him before he does any more damage."

"Right," she nodded, still looking at me as if this was all my fault.

I stepped outside, pulling out my phone to call Casey. "Hey, listen," I told him when he picked up, "I need you and Luke to go to *Malinda's Star* and stay aboard. We're gonna need some backup."

"Sure, but why?" Casey asked, confused.

"That treasure we found," I said, lowering my voice. "I buried it below *Malinda's Star* to keep it safe. I want you to call me if anyone approaches the boat. Got it?"

"Got it," he agreed, although still puzzled. I was doing this to keep him away from Brittany, his sister. There was no need to make this worse than it already was.

"Stay sharp, and don't hesitate to call me if anything happens," I warned.

"Will do, Cam," he promised before hanging up.

"Let's split up and search the area," I suggested to the others. "We can cover more ground that way."

"Be careful," Jack said, his eyes meeting mine in a silent understanding.

The hunt for Pedro was on, and I wouldn't rest until we found him—or he found us.

As night fell, we returned to my boat empty-handed and frustrated. Pedro had slipped through our fingers, and I couldn't shake the feeling that we were running out of time. The air was thick with tension as we boarded *The Same Old Song.*

"Cam," Kailey whispered, her hand on my arm, "We'll find him."

"Yeah, I know."

Just then, we heard footsteps approaching the boat. A trio of police officers stepped into the light of the dock, their expressions stern and serious.

"Mr. Derringer?" one of them asked, his voice firm. "We need to speak with you about the murders in Moctezuma."

"Of course," I replied, trying to maintain a calm façade. "What do you need to know?"

"According to witnesses, you were seen near the scene of the crime last night," the officer continued, his gaze unyielding.

"Pedro is the one who murdered those men," I explained. "He tried to blame me for it. But I was there to rescue Casey, not to kill anyone."

"Where is this 'Casey' now?" another officer interjected, suspicion etched across his face.

"Casey is aboard the boat," I said, gesturing toward *Malinda's Star*. "I sent him to keep watch."

"Cam," Brittany said. "What happened in Moctezuma?"

"Some of Pedro's men were killed. He sent me there just to set me up. Then he killed them and blamed it on me. But Jack was the one arrested by mistake."

The officers were looking more uncomfortable by the second. "They were about to kill him when Pedro called to tell them they had the wrong guy. I was holding a gun on Pedro at the time, so he convinced them to return Jack unharmed."

"That was not us," an officer said. "Those policemen were from the revolution. We would not do that."

"Regardless of who they were, the truth remains," I insisted. "Pedro is responsible for those murders, not me."

Brittany stepped forward, her eyes determined. "I want to go back to the office with you," she told the officers. "I think I can straighten this all out."

The officers exchanged glances and then nodded. "Alright, ma'am. We'll give it a try."

As Brittany left with the police, I couldn't help but worry about what would happen next. The entire situation was a tangled mess, and I feared that untangling it might prove difficult for even someone as resourceful as Brittany.

An hour passed. My thoughts raced, trying to come up with backup plans if Brittany's attempts failed. What would we do if the police didn't believe us? How could we prove Pedro's guilt?

Then, finally, I saw Brittany returning to the boat. Her face was unreadable, and my heart clenched with fear. Had she been successful in clearing our names?

"Cam," she said, her voice steady, "the problem with the police is gone."

"Really?" I asked, relief flooding through me. "How did you manage that?"

"Let's just say I have some connections," she replied cryptically, a small smile playing on her lips. "Anyway, we're in the clear now. We can focus on finding Pedro and putting an end to this nightmare."

"Thank you, Brittany," I said.

She gave me that look.

Chapter 32

The moon climbed high as we savored our drinks on the rear deck of my yacht. Jack, Kailey, Brittany, Rosalinda, Vinicio, and I were gathered there, discussing how best to find Pedro. Walter sat among us, ears perked up, waiting for a loving scratch behind them.

"Maybe we can ask around the local bars," suggested Jack, swirling his whiskey in his glass. "Someone's bound to have seen him."

"Or we could try tracking him down through his contacts," Kailey chimed in, her eyes darting between us.

Rosalinda shifted uncomfortably, her face tense. "I don't know if I can stay on this boat tonight. I need to be safe. I'm afraid Pedro will know I am with you and come after me."

"Hey, it's alright," Vinicio reassured her with a soft smile. "I have a hotel room nearby. You can stay there with me. You'll be safe, I promise."

"Thank you, Vinicio," she whispered, relieved.

"Whatever it takes. We're all in this together," I said.

"Cam's right," agreed Brittany, placing a comforting hand on Rosalinda's shoulder. "We'll find him, no matter what."

"Okay, let's split up and search," I decided. "Jack and Kailey, you check out the local bars. Brittany and I will work on Pedro's contacts. Vinicio, keep an eye on Rosalinda. If Pedro does come after her, you might be the one to encounter him."

"Hey," Rosalinda said, "are you using me for bait?"

"No, we're trying to keep you safe," I assured her.

"Let's call it a night then. We have a long day ahead of us tomorrow," I announced, finishing off my drink.

Vinicio helped Rosalinda stand up. "Come on, let's get you to the hotel," he said softly, his protective nature evident. They left the boat together, disappearing into the night.

"Stay safe, you two," Jack called after them as the rest of us prepared for the task ahead.

"Alright, guess I'll take the sofa tonight," Jack said, stretching his arms above his head.

"Jack, you can have the second bedroom," Brittany replied. "Cam knows I prefer to sleep with him and Kailey anyway."

"Are you sure?" Jack asked, a bit surprised by her offer.

"Of course, we insist," Kailey chimed in, a knowing smile playing on her lips.

"Thanks, then," Jack said, nodding appreciatively and heading to the second bedroom.

I couldn't help but feel a familiar excitement bubbling inside me as I watched Brittany and Kailey linger in the living area, exchanging glances and subtle touches that hinted at their intimate history. We'd all been through so much together, and these moments of closeness had become our way of coping with the dangers and uncertainties we faced. We've been together in the past, but I never really thought it would happen again. But it was fine with me.

"Shall we turn in as well?" I suggested.

"Absolutely," Brittany agreed, intertwining her fingers with mine. Kailey nodded, her eyes sparkling with anticipation.

As we made our way into the master bedroom, the tension between us was electric. It wasn't the first time we'd sought comfort in each other's arms—and it likely wouldn't be the last. In this unpredictable world, where danger lurked around every corner, we needed the solace that only our shared passion could provide.

We took turns in the shower and then settled into bed.

The night passed in a whirlwind of tangled limbs, whispered confessions, and feverish desire. It was an escape from the chaos outside our boat, a chance to reconnect and remind ourselves of what truly mattered: our love for one another and our determination to see justice served.

As dawn approached, we lay tangled in the sheets, our breathing finally slowing down. The challenges of the day ahead loomed large, but we knew we could face them together. After all, there was no force more powerful than the bond we shared.

My dreams were filled with the events of the day and the night, a chaotic mix of danger and desire. But suddenly, I was jolted awake. A faint sound from outside the bedroom had me on high alert.

"Did you hear that?" Brittany whispered, her voice tense. Kailey nodded, her eyes wide in the darkness.

We quickly got dressed, our hearts racing as we prepared to face whatever might be waiting for us beyond the door. I took the lead, my strong hand wrapped firmly around a flashlight. The beam cut through the shadows, revealing the empty hallway.

"Stay close," Jack told us, his voice barely audible. We followed him out onto the deck, our bare feet silent on the wooden planks.

"Who's there?" I demanded, the flashlight sweeping across the boat.

"Easy, Cam, it's just me," came a familiar voice. Silvio stepped out from behind one of the support beams, hands raised to show he meant no harm.

"Silvio, what the hell are you doing here?" I asked, trying to keep my anger in check. "You nearly got killed."

"Sorry, didn't mean to startle you guys. But I've got news," he replied, lowering his hands. "I know where Pedro is hiding."

"Where?" Cam asked, his tone all business now.

"Isla Holbox," Silvio replied. "It's a few hours away by car but faster by boat."

"Alright," I said, nodding. "Let's get moving then. No time to waste."

"This would be a good time to just leave," Jack said.

"Pedro would find us before we made it home. I don't want to go through that again. Besides, he has a lot of lives to pay for. Casey and

Luke still haven't found all of the treasure and they deserve a chance to finish what they've been working for."

"You're right, Cam. I just wanted to make sure we were on the same page."

I looked at the girls for conformation. "I'm not leaving until that son of a bitch is dead," Malinda said.

Kailey nodded, "Likewise."

As we gathered our things and prepared to set sail, I couldn't help but feel a strange sense of foreboding. As much as we wanted to find Pedro and bring him to justice, I knew the journey would be fraught with danger.

We stopped at Casey's boat first to let him know where we were headed. Brittany stayed below deck so he wouldn't see her.

The day was new, but Casey was sitting on the fantail drinking his morning coffee. He called out to me as I approached his starboard side.

"Good morning, all," he greeted.

We both dropped our bumpers over the side as I eased my boat to his.

"Just wanted to let you know we are going to Holbox. I had word that Pedro and some of his men were there. If we don't go to them, it won't be long before they come to us."

"It's just you, Jack, and Kailey?"

"That will be enough," I assured him. "We'll be discrete."

"I can get my gun and come with you," he said.

"We're good. We need you here."

Casey was silent for a minute. Then he spoke up, "Do you have time to help me get the duffel from the bottom and bring it up here?"

"Are you leaving?"

"Not until we take care of Pedro. Luke is still pretty sore. I owe it to him to get even. What if Jack stays here to watch him, and I go with you?"

"I can't do that, Casey," I said, thinking about Malinda sitting in the salon. "Jack and I have worked together as partners for a long time. We've been in worse situations and had each other's backs before. We'll come straight back here when we find Pedro."

"Call if you need me."

My tanks were full, and I didn't see why we needed to be in a hurry. Fifteen minutes wasn't going to make or break this mission.

I said, "Drop the line, and I'll attach the bag."

I put on my single tank and fins, then dropped into the clear blue water.

Visibility was perfect, and I found the bag immediately. I hooked the Carabiner Clip to the handle and swam to the surface.

That's when I saw the boat coming toward us.

Chapter 33

I could feel the salt in my eyes as I surfaced, gripping the side of my boat. The first thing I noticed was the approaching boat. Kailey and Jack glanced around cautiously, their eyes darting between me and the boat cutting through the water towards us.

"Cam, we have company?" Kailey shouted over the roar of the waves.

"Government boat," I replied, hauling myself onto the deck. "We need to get out of here."

"What about the treasure?" Jack asked.

"Casey, let it go," I yelled, meeting his gaze with steely determination. "It's not worth it if they catch us."

I saw Casey release the line, letting the treasure drift to the bottom once more.

The four of us exchanged anxious glances as the government boat closed in, its dark hull slicing through the azure sea. I could see the uniformed men aboard, their faces stern and authoritative. We couldn't outrun them, not with our two boats tied together.

"Everyone stay calm," I instructed, my voice firm. "We're just diving for old shipwrecks, nothing more. Got it?"

Kailey and Jack nodded in unison, their expressions a mix of tension and resolve. The government boat pulled alongside ours, and I took a deep breath.

"Ahoy there!" I called out, forcing a friendly smile onto my face. "Beautiful day for diving, isn't it?"

The men on the government boat exchanged wary glances before one of them stepped forward. He was tall and imposing, his uniform immaculate, and wore an expression that could curdle milk. Then another man appeared from their cabin. Even though the morning was already heating up, this man wore a white suit. He had politician written all over him. My guess was confirmed when he said, "I am

Pascual Duran. I will be the new mayor of Yucatan after the next election."

He's the bastard who tried to have Malinda killed.

"Nice to meet you," I lied.

"Señor," he sneered, revealing a row of yellowed teeth. "What business do you have in Mexican waters?"

"We're just diving old shipwrecks," I replied, trying to keep my voice steady. "Exploring the past, nothing more."

His eyes narrowed as they scanned our boats, lingering on Casey's vessel. "That looks like a treasure hunter's boat if I ever saw one."

"Maybe so," I conceded, fighting the urge to glance toward Brittany's hiding spot. "But we haven't found anything worth taking home yet. Just empty wrecks and fish."

"Empty wrecks and fish, huh?" The man leaned in closer, his cold gaze locked on mine. "You wouldn't mind if we took a look around then, would you?"

I swallowed hard, knowing that if they found Brittany, her life, but more than likely, their lives would be in immediate danger. But refusing their search would only arouse suspicion and put us all at risk.

"Of course not," I said, offering a stiff nod. "Help yourselves."

The uniformed men climbed aboard, their boots thudding heavily against the deck as they began their search. My heart raced with each passing second, praying that Brittany remained well-hidden.

Casey spoke up, attempting to ease the tension. "You're right about this being a treasure hunter's boat, señor," he said, his voice betraying a hint of nervousness. "But I must admit, we haven't had much luck. We did find a small treasure, but Pedro took it from us."

"Pedro?" Duran's eyes flashed with anger as a vein in his forehead bulged. "That scoundrel has no right!"

I could tell that Duran was furious about not getting a piece of the loot, and I hoped we could use this to our advantage.

"Pedro seems like a difficult man to trust," I offered cautiously, trying to stoke the flames of Duran's discontent. "If you ask me, it's best to keep an eye on someone like that."

"Indeed," Duran huffed, momentarily distracted from his search. "When I am mayor, men like him will be dealt with accordingly."

As the government men continued their search, my mind raced, trying to devise a plan if they found Brittany. But I was drawing a blank, and all I could do was watch helplessly as they rummaged through our belongings.

"Who is the man in the bed? He looks as if he has been wounded," Duran asked returning to the deck of Casey's boat.

I heard Casey tell him that Luke had been shot by Pedro as he stole our treasure.

"Pedro is getting out of hand. We will have a talk," Duran said.

Finally, after what felt like an eternity, Duran's men climbed back onto their boat without discovering anything incriminating. Relief washed over me as I watched them depart, leaving a wake of choppy water behind them.

"Safe travels," Duran called out mockingly as their boat sped away into the distance.

"Thanks," I muttered under my breath.

Wasting no time, I rushed inside my boat, desperate to find Brittany and ensure her safety. But she wasn't there. Panic set in as I scanned the cabin, and then I noticed the anchor chain in the water.

"Brittany!" I called out, my voice strained with worry. And there she was, climbing back onto the boat, her blonde hair slick and wet from hiding in the water. She offered me a small smile, her blue eyes filled with gratitude.

"Who's that?" Casey asked, his eyes wide with surprise.

Chapter 34

B rittany slipped into the cabin before Casey could get a good look at her. I watched her go, trying to gather my thoughts. I turned back to Casey and said, "Her name is Brittany. She had to hide because the man on that boat tried to have her killed yesterday. She's an extremely powerful figure in the Caribbean and poses a threat to him and his operation."

"I'd like to meet her," he said.

"Maybe later. She's getting in the shower, and we need to go."

"What about the treasure?"

"I think it's best to leave it where it is. These waters are full of sharks. The two-legged kind. We'll get it before we leave the area."

The sea was calm as our yacht cut through the water, sending frothy white waves cascading in our wake. The sun beat down on us, but there was a cool breeze to balance it out. Kailey, Brittany, and Jack joined me on the deck. We were making good time toward Holbox Island, where we hoped to find Pedro before he found us. The tension in the air was palpable, but we all tried to keep our minds occupied.

"Cam, what are we going to do about Brittany and Casey when this is over?" Kailey asked me secretly, her eyes scanning the horizon.

"I don't know. I guess we'll have to leave that up to Brittany. I sure would like to see the two of them get together again," I replied, gripping the wheel tighter. "This life chose them, not the other way around."

Brittany chimed in, her voice smooth like velvet, yet icy. I didn't think she could hear us, but she did. "I've been thinking about that too," she said. "I would love to have a small part of my family back." She looked at me sadly. I was once a part of her family. "I just don't know if I can."

Kailey hugged her. Their relationship was one of strength and sharing. I knew they both loved me, and I loved them as well. I consider myself the luckiest man in the world.

We turned and looked back out at the sea.

"Pedro doesn't stand a chance against us," Jack said, his hands flexing unconsciously, itching for action.

I nodded in agreement, though privately I couldn't help but worry about what we might find on the island. This wasn't just some small-time crook we were chasing; Pedro was as unpredictable as they came.

As we approached Holbox Island, I dropped anchor. We boarded the tender, each of us silent, focused on the task ahead. Walter jumped in last, wagging his tail and panting happily, oblivious to the danger lurking nearby.

Once ashore, we began our search for Pedro, traversing the colorful streets of the island town. Walter took an interest in a scruffy stray cat, engaging in a playful game of chase that ended with the cat perched atop a fence, hissing at the excited dog.

"What's gotten into Walter?" Jack chuckled, shaking his head.

"Everyone needs a little fun sometimes," I mused, watching the antics with a half-smile. "Even in the face of danger."

We continued our search, asking locals if they'd seen Pedro or anyone matching his description. No one seemed to know anything, but we pressed on, determined not to give up.

We eventually reached a part of the island where the atmosphere seemed to change. The locals here appeared more guarded, casting furtive glances at one another as we passed by. It was clear that something was amiss in this corner of paradise.

"Something's off," Kailey whispered, her eyes scanning the area with an unsettling intensity.

"Let's ask around," I suggested, hoping someone might break their silence and give us the lead we needed.

As we approached a group of fishermen mending their nets, I noticed one of them eyeing us nervously. He looked like he had something to say, but was too afraid to speak up.

"Excuse me," I said to him, trying to sound both friendly and authoritative. "We're looking for a man named Pedro. Have you seen him?"

The fisherman hesitated, his eyes darting back and forth between his companions, before finally settling on us. "Pedro... he was here earlier," he whispered, his voice barely audible over the sound of crashing waves. "He left not long ago."

"Which way did he go?" Jack asked urgently, his face hardening.

The fisherman pointed toward the western side of the island, where a dense jungle loomed ominously. "That way," he said, "but I wouldn't follow him if I were you."

"Thanks," I muttered distractedly.

"Alright, let's split up," I said, turning to face my companions. "Kailey and Brittany, you two head that way along the coast. Jack, you and Walter, come with me through the center of town. We'll cover more ground this way.

"Got it," they replied in unison, and we set off in our separate directions, prepared to face whatever dangers lay ahead.

"Cam, I don't like this," Jack whispered, his eyes darting from one shadow to another as we walked the narrow streets. "Everyone looks on edge."

"Stay alert and keep moving," I replied, my voice low and steady.

Walter trotted along beside us, his ears pricked forward and his nose working the air. Even he seemed tense, picking up on the atmosphere of unease that had settled over the island.

A woman was standing in her doorway as we passed. I stopped and smiled at her. "Excuse me," I said. "We're looking for a man named Pedro. Do you know him?"

"Yes, I know who he is. He was here a few minutes ago. He went that way," she said, pointing down the street."

"Thank you, ma'am," I said, nodding my gratitude.

We pushed forward, each step bringing us closer to Pedro—or so I hoped.

"Cam," Jack said, "I think we should call Kailey and Brittany. Update them on what we've found."

"Good idea," I agreed, pulling out my phone and dialing Kailey's number. The line clicked, and her voice came through, tense but focused.

"Cam? What's the situation?"

"Pedro entered the center of town and is heading west," I relayed. "Jack, Walter, and I are following his trail. How about you two?"

"Nothing solid yet," Kailey replied, her voice tight with frustration. "But we'll keep searching along the coast."

"Stay safe and keep in touch," I said before hanging up.

"Let's go," I said, and at the same time, we heard a shot ring out.

Chapter 35

We felt the bullet whiz past us and heard it hit the building behind us. Walter was the first to take off running for cover. Jack and I were right behind him. Before we found a safe place to take cover, three more shots were fired in our direction.

The tourists and locals alike were running in all directions. We found safe refuge beside a restaurant. The concrete walls protected us from the bullets. I pulled my gun and double-checked my ammo. I was good. Jack nodded that he was the same.

"Pedro?" he asked as we crouched together beside the building. I could feel Walter's hot breath on my neck. He's been in a few of these gun fights and doesn't like it any more than I do.

I checked behind us for an escape route. We could go behind the building and try to flank them, but it was risky. The streets were narrow, and it would be easy to get trapped. I turned back to Jack and shook my head. "I don't think we can take them head-on," I said. "We need to find another way to get to Pedro."

Kailey and Brittany had heard the shots and came to where we were hiding. They were hiding behind a car a few feet away from us. Kailey looked pissed off, and Brittany seemed to be in control of the situation. "We need to split up," she said, her voice low and urgent. "Cam, you and Jack go one way, and Kailey and I will go the other. We'll try to draw their fire and create a diversion."

I hesitated for a moment but then nodded. It was a risky move, but we didn't have many options. We split up as planned, Jack and I taking one street and Kailey and Brittany taking another. We ran as fast as we could, dodging behind cars and buildings. Bullets whizzed past us and shattered windows.

I heard Jack curse beside me as a bullet grazed his arm. "Are you okay?" I asked as we ducked behind a car. "I'm fine," he grunted. "Let's keep moving." We made our way down the street, taking turns shooting at the men. I looked back and saw Walter about a half block behind us but still coming in our direction. He was hugging the protection of the buildings as he advanced. I motioned for him to stop. I didn't want to take an unnecessary chance of him getting hit. He paused but then moved toward us again.

Pedro and his men had the advantage over all of us. They would fire when they had a shot, but we didn't want to accidentally hit any of the tourists.

Then we heard a volley of gunshots coming from ahead. The bullets weren't coming toward us. "That must be Kailey and Brittany," I said. "Let's get there and help them."

Jack and I ran toward the gunshots. As we drew closer, we saw a few of Pedro's men lying in the street. Shots were still being fired from a building on our right and from behind a shed across the street.

"Kailey's behind that shed," I said after catching a glimpse of her. Then shots were being fired from the top of a building behind Kailey. "There's Brittany. That must be Pedro's gang in the building on the right."

"I'll work my way around the building and try to take them from behind," Jack said.

"Stay out of a cross-fire. Signal Brit when you get in position."

"Will do."

"Go on three, and I'll cover you," I said.

We counted to three, and Jack made his run. I stood and fired five shots toward the building's windows. Jack made it behind the buildings without getting shot at.

Brittany and Kailey stopped shooting when they saw Jack run behind the building. I moved slowly along the row of buildings making my way toward the one they were in. When I was two buildings away, my phone buzzed. I signaled the girls and made a run for the building.

Gunfire was raging inside the building now. Jack must have made his way in. Two men ran out the front door, firing wildly. Two pops from across the street, and both men fell.

When I reached the building, I dove through the front door and began firing at anyone who wasn't Jack. I dropped two men as soon as I entered. I could see another in the dark corner.

He hollered, "No, no," and threw his gun across the floor. There was no one else in the room.

Then I heard more shots down the street, moving to the edge of town. Jack must be after Pedro. I jumped up and ran out the back door, making my way quickly toward the gunfire.

The shooting stopped for a few seconds as I turned a corner. Then all hell broke loose. Pedro walked out into the street and opened up in Jack's direction with an automatic rifle. I saw Jack dive behind an old stack of boards. The boards were splintering from the gunfire. I hollered at Pedro. When he swung around, I already had my gun aimed at his chest. I was about fifty feet away but knew I could take him. He raised his rifle toward me, and I fired three shots into his chest. He fell to the ground, holding the trigger down. His bullets flew harmlessly into the air toward the Jungle behind him.

Then all was silent except for the police running toward us, yelling for us to drop our guns.

I dropped my gun and raised my hands in the air. Then I saw Jack stand from behind the wood stack, his hands in the air as well.

Two police held their guns on us as the other walked to where Pedro lay. He bent down and inspected the body. When he stood, he grinned and told his men to lower their guns. "It's Pedro!" He called to them.

Kailey and Brittany walked up to the scene, their guns nowhere in sight, but I knew they were on them somewhere.

I felt relief run through my body as I looked at Pedro lying in the mud. A fitting ending for him, for sure.

I knew our troubles were far from over. Pascual Duran was still out there, and now he thought we might have treasure. I wondered if he would be angry because we killed Pedro.

The police took our names and asked a few questions about where we were staying and what our business was in the area. When they got to Brittany, I saw one of them tap the other. He whispered something in his ear. The captain, who was in charge, then stood straight and told us to have a nice day. "If you need anything, be sure to give us a call personally."

We thanked them and turned to leave just as Walter made his appearance from behind a snack bar. He had a wrapper from something he had found sticking out of the corner of his mouth.

"Are you ready to go, boy?" I asked him.

He turned and walked along beside us. His big day was almost over. The sun was working its way down now, casting long shadows.

The townspeople and tourists watched us as we made our way back to the tender we had left at the pier. I saw a lot of phones being held up. We were going to be the talk of many people's vacation. Kailey and Brittany hid their faces as best they could. In their line of work, publicity wasn't a good thing.

It felt good to climb aboard *The Same Old Song* again. The first thing we did was make drinks, sit down at the table, and down them.

"Another?" Kailey asked.

I went to the bar and brought the bottle and a bucket of ice to the table.

"Go for it," I said as I watched the sky turn pink and orange. It was going to be a beautiful sunset.

Kailey noticed Jack's arm. "You're hit."

"It's nothing."

She went inside and returned with the first aid kit. After doing an excellent job of cleaning and covering the flesh wound, she kissed it. "Now it's all better," she said.

Chapter 36

I called Casey and told him about our adventure in Holbox. Then I told him that we were going to spend the night anchored off the coast and would head back in the morning.

I removed four steaks from the fridge and lit the Green Egg. Kailey cleaned and placed potatoes in the microwave while Malinda made a salad. Jack fed and played with Walter.

We had a peaceful evening talking about what had happened a little, but mostly about what was to come.

Malinda said she was going to contact her team and have them find Pascual Duran.

"What will you do about him?" I asked her.

"We'll try to reason with him first. If that doesn't work..."

"He sounds like a crooked politician. Why would you want to reason with him?"

"He has some value to the region. But since he tried to kill me, I'm not sure my team will let him live."

"What could he possibly do for the people here?"

"He controls a lot of resources and has a lot of connections. If we can get him on our side, we can make a big difference in the lives of the people here," Malinda explained.

I nodded thoughtfully, and we all fell into a comfortable silence as we ate our dinner and watched the sunset. After dinner, we sat around the table drinking and talking. Eventually, Kailey and Jack excused themselves and went to bed, leaving Malinda and me to enjoy the night.

As the night wore on, the conversation turned to more personal topics. Malinda and I found ourselves talking about our past relationships and what we wanted in the future.

"I want to be a part of Casey's life again," she said.

"Is that possible?"

"It could be if I worked it right. I would have a lot of explaining to do, though. I'm not sure he would understand."

"If you decide that's what you want, we'll face him together. I'll talk to him first so he won't be totally shocked when he sees you."

"I'll sleep on it tonight, and maybe by the time we see him tomorrow, I'll know what to do."

I leaned in and kissed her. "Whatever you decide, we're all here for you."

"I know. I'm a lucky girl."

Malinda and I went to the bedroom to find Walter curled in the bed next to Kailey. I tapped him on the shoulder. He pretended not to feel me. With a little coaxing, he finally got out of bed and lay on the floor on Kailey's side.

We took off our clothes and climbed in next to her. Kailey turned toward me, kissed me, and then fell back to sleep. Malinda wrapped her arms around me from behind and fell asleep, too. I lay awake thinking about how tomorrow was going to go.

The morning glow filtered through the blinds, casting shadows on the three of us. Looking to my left and right, I saw nothing but naked women. However, the day ends, it has had a perfect start.

I carefully climbed over Kailey and slipped my shorts on. I found Jack sitting on the rear deck drinking coffee.

"Good morning," he said cheerfully.

"Morning, Jack. How'd you sleep?"

"Like a baby. I think we wore ourselves out yesterday."

"I agree."

"I called Diane when I got in bed last night. She said to tell you she loves you."

I smiled. "How much did you tell her?"

"Everything."

"And?"

"She already knew most of it. Kailey had been keeping her informed. Diane's the one who put the bug in their ear about checking up on us."

"I should have known."

I relayed the conversation Malinda and I had last night.

"Wow, that could go either way."

"Yeah, I think seeing him yesterday might have brought up some old feelings. She misses having a family. I'm going to talk to him later today and see how he would feel if she would miraculously show up again."

I felt something wet on my leg. I looked down and saw Walter licking me. "Good morning," I said and rubbed his head.

"I guess we should fix the girls breakfast. They had a hard day yesterday," Jack said.

"That they did, but they also had steaks last night."

"True," he said and thought a few seconds. "How about I bake a coffee cake?"

"Perfect. There's a box in the pantry."

Malinda and Kailey appeared as the coffee cake was coming out of the oven.

"Ooh, that smells good," Kailey said.

"Yeah, we had to lay in bed for a half hour waiting for you to get it out of the oven," Malinda chimed in.

"This is for the guys," I said. "There's cereal in the pantry for you two."

"We'll see about that," Kailey said. "You two go on outside and we'll bring the cake after we cut it. Take the milk with you."

Jack and I went outside and waited for our cake and waited and waited. "I'd better go check on 'em," Jack said.

He got up and went to the door, but it was locked. He cupped his hands to the glass. "They're in there eating the coffee cake," he shouted.

I stood next to him and cupped my hands, too. The girls turned and waved at us. They each had half a cake on their plates, and it didn't look as if they were going to save us any.

I looked down and saw Walter had his face against the door, too. He looked up at me as if to say, "Do something."

Malinda disappeared into the kitchen, then I saw her taking the steps up to the flybridge. *What the heck?*

"Hey, boys," I heard her voice from above us. "Here ya go."

I looked up just in time to catch the cereal box that she dropped toward us. Then she was gone.

I looked at Jack as he looked at the box. "Really," he said, "Fruit Loops?"

The door slid open a few minutes later. "Thanks, guys," Malinda said. "That was just what we needed."

"Why did you do that?" I asked.

"Do what?"

"Eat all the cake."

"Did you want some?"

I looked at Jack again. He was looking at me. "You're the funny one who said they weren't going to get any."

"I was just kidding."

"Oh, I'm sorry," Malinda said. "I wish I'd known that was the only one you made."

She stepped back inside and closed the door.

"Good job, Cam," Jack said, looking at the cereal box. "Got a bowl?"

We opened the door and stepped inside with Walter at our heels. Kailey was standing in the kitchen, putting their plates in the dishwasher. "Hi, guys," she said cheerfully. "Thanks for the cake."

Malinda said, "We were supposed to share it, it seems."

"Oh, no," Kailey retorted.

"That's okay, girls," I said. "I guess you needed it."

Kailey raised two plates from the galley counter. "What do you want me to do with your half, then?" she asked.

They both laughed. Jack and I devoured our half of the cake. Walter got his fair share.

It was going to be a beautiful day.

Chapter 37

Casey worked on his equipment as the sun was rising from the eastern sky. Now that Pedro was gone, he would be free to dive *The Tide* and also recover the gold and silver they already had found.

Luke sat in a dock chair and busied himself blowing out the air tanks and cleaning the regulators. Casey had done it the night before but wanted Luke to feel like he was helping.

"It looks to be a beautiful day," Luke said. "The sun will feel good on my skin. I think I'll be able to dive by tomorrow."

Casey gave him a glance, "We'll see," but Casey knew he wouldn't be able to dive for at least a week.

He kept an eye on the horizon for *The Same Old Song* as he put the DPVs on charge. *I wonder if today will be the day?*

Then he heard a boat engine from behind him. It was the same boat as yesterday. Pascual Duran's stocky figure stood on the bow as the boat turned slightly to come up on their port.

"Luke, we've got company."

Luke looked up and frowned. "What the hell now?" He reached down below his chair and picked up the nine-millimeter gun that he had put there earlier. He stuck it in his belt and pulled his shirt down over it.

Casey watched as Pascual Duran's boat docked next to *Malinda's Star*. He could see the greed in Duran's eyes as he stepped onto the boat with two of his henchmen in tow.

"Hola, my friend," Duran said with a smirk. "I hear you've been busy."

"What do you want, Duran?" Casey asked, his hand hovering over the harpoon gun nearby.

Duran's smirk widened. "I want what's mine. You know what I'm talking about."

"If you mean the treasure we found and rightfully own, Pedro already took it. I don't owe you anything," Casey said, his voice low and threatening.

Duran's henchmen stepped forward, but Luke held up his gun, aiming it at them. "Back off," he growled.

Duran chuckled. "You think that gun scares me?" He pulled out his own weapon, a shiny silver revolver. "I have a better one. And I have more men waiting on the shore."

Casey lifted the harpoon and pointed it at Duran. "One of us will kill you. No matter what you do," Casey said calmly.

Duran's eyes darted between Luke's gun and the harpoon. He smiled and put his gun away. He held his hands out. "Gentlemen, we can come to an agreement. There is no reason for anyone to get hurt here. We will go now and let you get back to treasure hunting. But we will be back for our share, let's say," he paused a bit, "Sixty percent."

"Zero percent," Casey said. "Now get the hell out of here."

Duran stepped back onto his boat. He turned to Casey. "Where are your friends?"

"They're around."

"It seems they have been very busy in Holbox. Pedro is no more."

"Good riddance," Casey growled. "He won't be missed."

Duran stared at Casey for a minute, then smirked. "Let's go," he told his men. "See you soon!" he called to Casey as they sped away.

"Out of the pan and into the fire," Luke said.

"We're not giving any more of our treasure up," Casey said as he leaned the harpoon back against the bulkhead.

He looked back toward the eastern horizon. She might be his only chance.

• • • •

I PULLED THE BOAT AHEAD a little to break the anchor loose while Jack stood by the winch. When I felt it give. I signaled to him, and he flipped the switch.

We started our short cruise back toward El Cuyo. Malinda joined me in the pilothouse.

"Have you given any thought to Casey today?" I asked her when she sat beside me on the double captain's chair.

"Yes, I want him to know," she said as she searched my face for reassurance.

"That's what I hoped you would say."

I could see her shoulders drop and her face relax. It looked as though a heavy burden had been lifted, and I think it had.

She was silent as she lay her head on my shoulder. I hoped this was the start of a new life for her. I wondered how our life would be if justice hadn't taken her away from me.

An hour later, I nudged her awake. "Casey's boat," I said.

I saw her tense up again. "Relax," I said. "I'll talk to him first."

She nodded and took the steps to the salon. She would stay out of sight until I had a chance to talk to Casey.

"Ahoy," Casey called as we approached.

I dropped my anchor about 100 yards from him and waited for him to come to get us in his tender, which was already in the water.

Casey stepped onboard and glanced around at us. "Where's Brittany?" He asked.

"Holbox," I said. "She had some things to finish up."

"Oh, too bad." Casey looked disappointed.

"Well, I had another visit from Duran. It looks like he wants to pick up where Pedro left off," Casey said.

"I thought that might happen. Brittany knows him pretty well. She said he was no good, but could be an advantage to the people in the area."

"Maybe they can get someone else to help them. I think Duran needs to leave the area and never return."

"You're probably right," I said, while thinking over the situation. "You do have all the permits to dive here and look for treasure, don't you?" I asked.

"Yes, sir. That was the first thing I did when we arrived."

"Good, at least we have the Mexican government on our side. My guess is these guys try to shake down everyone who comes here to dive. Especially with a salvage boat as nice as yours."

Casey looked back at his boat with pride. "Yeah, it is a good one."

Malinda's Star gleamed in the morning sun, the two-foot letters telling the world her name.

"Would you like to go to town with me?" I asked. "I have a few things to pick up. They'll watch Luke for you while we're gone."

"Sure, let 'em get their stuff together, and we'll go."

"They can go in my tender. Then if they need to return before we get back, they'll have a boat."

"We'll be alright," Jack said. "You guys go on, and I'll get Kailey. We'll see ya in a few hours."

Casey and I got in his boat and turned toward El Cuyo. Mario was standing on the dock waiting for us. I threw him the line, and he tied us off.

Tito came running to us when he saw who had arrived. "Mister Casey, Mister Cam, welcome back," he said excitedly. "Do you have any treasures?"

"Not today, Tito," Casey said. "We've been too busy the last few days."

"I told you they were fighting, Pedro," Mario said. "With my dad." He puffed out his chest.

"We're going into town to get some supplies and a bite to eat," I told the boys. "Fill up the tank."

Mario ran to the pumps while Tito pulled the boat to the dock next to him. We made our way to the heart of town.

"You wanna beer?" I asked. I could feel my blood racing through my veins. My nerves were on edge now, thinking of a way to talk to Casey about Malinda.

"He looked at me a little funny but said, "Yeah, sure."

We went to Naia Cafe and took a table outside. We ordered two beers and sat silently.

"What's up, Cam?"

I took a deep breath and let it out. "Well, seeing you has made me think about Malinda. I really miss her a lot."

"So do I, Cam. But don't you think she's in a good place?"

"A good place? Maybe. I think she would be in a better place if she were here with us."

"So do I. If there was any way to bring her back into our lives, I would be willing to do what it takes," Casey said, staring me in the eyes. "Anything."

He gave me the strange feeling that he thought I might have the ability to bring her back into his life.

"Yeah, me too," I said, putting off telling him about her. I took another swallow of my beer. A large swallow.

I sat the bottle down on the table and stared out into town.

"Cam, I'm going to make this easy for you because we don't have all day," he said.

"Easy for me?" I questioned.

"Yeah, I saw Malinda three years ago. I was in Nassau. I didn't approach her because she had what looked to me like bodyguards with her. I asked some locals, "Who is that beautiful woman?" They told me her name is Brittany and she's a very powerful person. So, I did some investigating. I know a lot about her. I've been back a few times to check on her. I figured if there was any way she could contact me, she would have. One time, while I was watching her, I saw you pick her up and take her back to your boat. I know she's out there right now, on your boat. Is that close to what you wanted to tell me?"

I couldn't even talk. I took another drink of my beer and nodded at the waitress to bring another.

"That's exactly what I was going to tell you. She wants to meet you again. She wants you to be a part of her life. But I have to warn you. Her life is very dangerous. She has ties to everything that happens in the Caribbean. If the wrong people knew you were her brother, your life and hers would be in jeopardy. That's one reason I'm not with her either."

"Aren't you in love with Kailey?"

"Yes, I am. But I love Malinda too. It's complicated."

My beer arrived, and I took another big swallow. Casey downed his beer, too.

"Sir, would you like another beer?" the waitress asked him.

"No, thank you. I have something important to do." He looked at me. "Are you ready?"

I paid the tab and we walked back to the tender.

"You forgot your supplies," Mario said when he saw us arrive empty-handed.

"We'll be back," I said.

Chapter 38

J ack pulled the skiff to the dive platform of the *Malinda's Star* and tied it off. He stepped onto the platform and then reached out for Kailey's hand. He helped her onboard, then reached for Malinda.

"Good morning," Luke said as they all walked to the deck.

"Morning, Luke," Jack said. "This is Brittany,"

Luke went to Brittany and hugged her. "It's so good to finally meet you," he said.

Brittany was slightly taken aback. "Thanks, it's nice to meet you too."

She looked at Jack, who just shrugged his shoulders.

"Casey and Cam should be returning shortly," Luke said. "Have a seat."

Brittany sat nervously in her chair while she watched the horizon for the tender to return.

"Brittany," Luke said. "Are you okay?" He had noticed how tense she seemed to be.

"I'm fine, thank you."

"Casey has been wanting to meet you for some time now."

Brittany looked at Luke, puzzled. "He knows?"

Luke slowly nodded his head.

Brittany turned and stared toward El Cuyo. She took a deep breath and let it out. "Good."

Her vision was jarred by the sight of the tender cutting through the water toward them. She stood and walked to the railing, watching as the boat bumped the platform.

• • • •

I GOT OUT FIRST, AND then Casey stepped onto the boat. He turned to face Malinda. Their eyes locked on one another.

Casey walked to her. They embraced. Brittany's shoulders were shaking as she cried, hugging him tighter. Then Casey cried. Everyone else was silent, but tears trickled down our faces as well.

I stepped beside Kailey and put my arm around her. We remained silent until Malinda broke away from Casey and held his face in her hands. She turned to look at us and said, "This is my brother."

I stepped toward them and hugged them both. "Thank God that part is over," I said.

Kailey and Jack took their turns hugging the couple. We were happy for Malinda, who had been alone for so long. Now she had a brother she could call and talk to about—anything.

Malinda and Casey sat on a bench and talked while the rest of us made plans to recover the treasure we had left below.

"Once we get it onboard, we'll move back to *The Tide* and dive it again. I'll stay here for as long as they need me. Jack, if you need to get back to Key West, we'll be okay."

"I've taken care of business there. Diane is checking on the boat, and Ronnie is taking my clients out. I'm in for the long haul."

"Thanks, Jack."

"Then let's suit up," I said.

"How deep is the treasure?" Kailey asked.

"Right here it's only about thirty feet," I told her.

Kailey pulled her clothes off, revealing a skimpy swimsuit, which she removed. She grabbed the line and said, "I'll be right back." She dove over the side and disappeared.

"Well, we won't live this one down for a while," Jack said.

"I was just thinking the same thing."

A minute later, Kailey broke the surface and took a deep breath. "It's hooked up. Do you want me to come up there and pull it up, or do you boys think you can get it together?"

"We can handle it," I said, witnessing the first of the many digs coming our way.

Then, if things weren't bad enough, Malinda picked up the line and pulled the duffle to the surface.

I ran to her and said, "Let me help get it into the boat."

It did take the two of us to land it on the deck. It was much heavier and full of water once we got it out of the ocean.

"Thank you so much for the assistance," she said as the bag thudded to the deck.

"Don't you two have some cooking or cleaning to do?" I asked loud enough for Kailey to hear, too.

"Not me," she said. "I'm going to go back down and get us a fish for supper."

I leaned over the side to make another comment. That's when I was pushed from behind and plunged into the water next to Kailey.

When I surfaced, I saw Malinda laughing above me. "You'll be sorry for that one, girl," I yelled.

She pulled her clothes off, but there was no suit on her, and dove into the water with us. Now I had to make nice. I was in the water with two women I was not sure I could overpower.

Kailey hooked her arms around me from behind while Malinda pulled my clothes off and flung them onto the boat.

Walter thought it was amusing. He ran around the deck barking until he took the plunge and landed next to us. He swam in circles around us for a minute then, getting tired, he came to me and put his paws on my shoulders. Now I had to try to tread water with a seventy-pound wet golden retriever hanging on me.

I swam to the platform, where I pushed Walter onto the boat. He shook the water off, then ran to the upper deck and jumped into the sea again.

"You're on your own this time," I told him.

As I looked around, I realized that Malinda and Kailey were nowhere to be seen. I called out to them, but there was no answer. Panic set in as I realized that I was alone in the open sea with no idea where they had gone. I started to swim toward the boat, hoping that they had already climbed aboard. Suddenly, I felt a hand on my leg, and I turned around to see Kailey grinning at me mischievously. "Gotcha!" she exclaimed before diving back under the water. Relief washed over me as I realized that they were just playing a prank on me. I laughed and swam after Kailey, catching her around the waist and pulling her close to me. We shared a long, deep kiss, the saltwater mixing with our tongues as we explored each other's mouths. Malinda surfaced beside us, grinning widely. "Looks like you two are having fun," she said before diving back down into the water. Kailey and I continued to kiss, our bodies entwined in the warm, salty water. I could feel her breasts pressed against my chest, her nipples hardening in response to my touch. I was pressing against her thigh as we continued to kiss passionately. Suddenly, I felt a sharp pain in my leg, and I jerked away from Kailey, trying to see what had bitten me. She looked at me and giggled before swimming away. Malinda surfaced next to me, and I realized that she had just given me a love bite, and I smiled at her in return, following her as she swam towards the boat. Kailey was waiting for us.

We climbed aboard, and I pulled myself to my feet. She giggled again, and we shared another deep kiss.

Jack threw me a towel and told me to cover up.

"What about us?" Kailey said.

"We're out of towels," he answered, smiling broadly.

I went inside, leaving them out there on the deck naked with Jack, Casey, and Luke. A few seconds later, Kailey entered the stateroom I was using to dry off and dress.

I tossed her onto the bed, and as she bounced, I dropped the towel and climbed on top of her. Our bodies writhed against each other, our skin sticking together as we continued to kiss. I could feel myself sliding between her legs. I groaned as I slid into her, her body clenching around me as I thrust myself inside her.

We loved passionately, our bodies entwined in the bed as the waves rocked the boat. She reached up and kissed me as I pushed myself in and out of her. She licked my ear and whispered into it. " I love you," she said, her breath tickling my ear. I groaned and pushed myself deeper inside of her.

"I love you too," I whispered back as we continued to kiss.

Finally, ending our lovemaking together, I slid off her and lay panting next to her.

"That was incredible," Kailey said, climbing out of the bed. She smiled at me and winked. I blushed and grinned back at her.

Malinda poked her head into our cabin. "Come on! Let's dance!" she said, before disappearing back outside.

We dressed and joined them on deck.

Malinda was playing with the radio, trying to find a station that she liked. "Ah! Here we go!" she exclaimed happily, turning up the volume.

"Damn! That sounds good," Kailey said, walking over to the speakers and turning the volume up even louder.

I lay on the deck, letting the music wash over me. Malinda and Kailey danced, laughing as they twirled and sang.

Chapter 39

The day was wasted with music and drinks. The grilled salmon for supper topped the evening off. Malinda and Casey grew closer as they told stories from their childhood.

"Are you going to tell Mom and Dad that you're still alive?" Casey asked.

"They know. Dad is the one who got me into this life to begin with. He thought he was doing the right thing. I've seen them a few times in locations far from where they live."

The next morning, Casey woke up to the smell of something cooking. He looked at the clock and saw that it was 8:30. He rolled out of bed and walked to the galley to see what was going on. Looking in, he saw Malinda standing at the stove, cooking up some eggs and bacon. She turned around and smiled at Casey.

"Good morning, sleepyhead," she teased. "I'm making breakfast. What can I get ya?"

Casey sat down at the table. "Just some coffee for now, I guess. Where is everyone?"

"They're on *The Same Old Song*. Luke went with them. They're going into town again today to get supplies. This time, they really are going to get supplies."

"I hope they don't run across Duran."

"If they do, they'll be able to handle him and his henchmen," Malinda said.

"I hope so. I've been thinking, maybe we should take what we have and leave."

"You're welcome to leave any time you wish," she said. "But now it's personal for me. I have some assistants on the way. Duran might be sorry he tried to kill me and extort you. I'll try to handle this civilized first, but one wrong move, and he's finished."

"You really do lead a dangerous life, don't you?"

"Sometimes," she said sadly. "Here's your coffee, and here are some bacon and eggs. Eat up. You have a big day ahead of you."

Casey ate his breakfast as he watched his sister work in the galley. He was proud of her and glad that they were finally back together where they belonged.

Then he started to think about Duran and how he would handle him. He couldn't do it alone. Malinda said she would handle it herself, but he still needed to be prepared to help her.

"Are we going to town with them today?" he asked.

"I thought we'd stay out here and keep an eye on the boats. We're going to move back to *The Tide* when they return."

"Good, I'm anxious to see what else we can find down there. The boat is in exceptional condition for being down there so long. Reports say there is a lot more gold than what we've found."

"One step at a time," Malinda cautioned. "If we have reason to believe the ship needs to be moved, I know of a company that can do it."

Casey perked up at the prospect. He hadn't given much thought to moving the boat. His own boat could move *The Tide* a little, but it wasn't quite big enough to move it away from its resting place entirely.

Their conversation was interrupted by Luke stepping into the galley. "They're on their way to El Cuyo," he said. "I thought I should stay here with you two."

"Sit down then and eat," Malinda said.

"I already did an hour ago," he said, looking at Casey.

"I'm sorry," Casey said. "I must have been tired. I think I needed the rest."

"There's one more thing I need to warn the two of you about," Malinda said.

They looked at her, waiting for the other shoe to drop.

"From now on, you refer to me as Brittany. No one knows my real name or where I come from. You can never tell anyone that I'm your sister. Are we clear on that?"

They both nodded their heads. "Got it, Brittany," Luke said. Then she looked at Casey. "I promise," he said.

"Good, now you guys can clean the kitchen," she said and went out to the deck with Walter.

Luke said, "You clean the galley. I didn't eat anything."

· · · ·

WE WALKED THROUGH THE town, working our way in and out of street markets, picking fresh fruit and vegetables. Jack was carrying a cooler. We were going to get some fresh fish before we left.

We ended up at *Abarrotes y Fruteria*, where we found everything we needed. They had a good assortment of fruit, veggies, and snacks. We gathered our supplies, paid, and stepped out into the tropical sun again.

"Fish," Kailey said.

"We'll get those at the docks from one of the fishermen," I said.

"Then why did I have to carry this cooler around town with me?" Jack asked.

"I don't know," I answered.

"Payback is a mother," he said.

"Ah, Señor, just the man I wanted to see," Duran said from behind me. Then Kailey stepped out of the store.

His eyes widened as he took in her long black hair and shapely figure. "Hello, señorita," he said, his smile widening.

She didn't respond, only gave him a look that made him hesitate.

"What do you want, Pascual?" I asked, hearing the annoyance in my tone.

"Only to say hello," he responded but still didn't take his eyes off Kailey.

"Stay away from Casey and *Malinda's Star*," I warned.

"These are my waters. I will go where I please," he responded, then dipped his head toward Kailey, "It's good to see you again, señorita."

He turned and walked down the street, leaving a foul taste in my mouth. Our day would come. I was sure of that.

Mario guided us to the best fisherman in the marina. There were several people standing around his boat, waiting for their turn to choose their fish. We bought three large red snappers and placed them in the cooler of ice.

As we cut through the waves heading back to *Malinda's Star*, I thought about Duran. I wouldn't like the man even if he wasn't trying to steal Casey's treasure. I knew that Malinda wasn't finished with him. I also wondered what he would do if he knew Brittany was on board with us. Did he know where she had escaped to? Was he watching his back?

I hoped he was nervous about her. I was looking forward to the two of them meeting again.

We climbed aboard and put the groceries away. Luke and Casey had the boat buttoned up and ready to move it over *The Tide* again. It was only a mile away, but the storm brewing in the distance promised to make our trip a little rocky.

Jack, Kailey, Walter, and I rushed around *The Same Old Song*, coiling ropes, affixing rain covers to the hatches, and raising anchor. As the rain pelted us with its icy drops, we all breathed a sigh of relief that we had made it back in time. I remained under cover until the storm weakened and then stepped out onto the deck. The salty air mingled with the promise of adventure as I looked up into the ever-lightening sky. With each droplet that splashed against my skin, I felt the tension from Duran drift away.

Chapter 40

We settled over the marker we had tied to *The Tide*.

Jack geared up to dive with Casey and me, and then at the last minute, Malinda and Kailey decided they were going too.

They were all experienced divers, and I thought, the more, the merrier.

We dropped into the water and descended to the wreck. Again, the condition of the boat amazed me. It didn't look like it had been here for two hundred years.

I hoped for Casey's sake that we would find more treasure, even though the treasure we had already found was worth a fortune. We split up when we reached the wreckage.

I headed for the stern when I saw a large metal barrel wedged in the corner. I swam over for a closer look. It was a large container, like the ones they would have stored whale oil in.

I tried to pull it loose, but it was jammed tight. I felt around the barrel and found the lid. It was closed, but it was also cracked, and I could tell that water had seeped into the container. I wondered if it was the only one.

I looked around for Jack and Casey and spotted them near the bow. Jack was using a crowbar to pry a hatch off. We had seen it earlier, but we weren't equipped to remove it.

Casey was right behind him, calling out the remaining air supply at regular intervals.

Jack stopped and turned to me. I swam to him and helped pry the hatch.

I hope this is it. The lid's coming loose too easily.

Casey swam over to the hatch Jack was standing over.

Together, we pulled the hatch open and peered inside. With the flashlight, we could see a whole new compartment we hadn't known about. It was unexplored and might be holding something valuable.

The problem was the hatch was too small to squeeze through. Even if Kailey took off her tank, she wouldn't fit. I knew we were going to have to move *The Tide* if not raise it completely. If the lid came off that easily, it had probably been open before.

I swam along, camera in hand, capturing images of the decaying wreck. As I passed a large hole in the stern, I spotted something out of the corner of my eye. At first, I thought it was merely a shadow. But then I noticed a dark mouth open and close slowly inside. Rocks had tumbled from the bilges to form an area darker than the rest of the deck around it.

My heart skipped a beat as I realized what it was—a great white shark, one of the largest I'd seen in these waters. I signaled to Casey and Jack while steadily backing away, never taking my eyes off the beast until it emerged from its hiding spot and moved gracefully past us. We watched in awe as I filmed it for posterity before we began exploring the wreck further, making mental notes of all that would need to be done in order to move it.

I made another pass around the boat as I filmed all of the areas I thought we could connect lines to.

I pointed to the surface. Kailey and Malinda were beside me as we slowly drifted up. Jack and Casey finished their assessment and joined us as we broke the surface.

Once onboard, we talked first about the size of the shark. Then we started to discuss what it would take to move or raise *The Tide*.

"I know some guys who would bring it to the surface," Malinda said.

"I'll give it a shot first," Casey said, looking down into the water as if he could see it from here. "Maybe we just need to turn it over a bit."

"How long would it take to hook it up and move it?" I asked Casey.

"A day."

"Or two," Luke said. "It depends on how stuck it is in the bottom. If it's totally embedded in the coral, it could pull us down before we could pull it up."

"True," Casey said. "It could be dangerous no matter how you look at it."

"Is there another way to get inside and search for more treasure?" I asked.

"Sure, we could cut a hole in the bulkhead, but what if the real treasure is under the ship? That can happen. Sailors have been known to panic and grab all the loot they can carry when a ship is going down. It sometimes is the end of them."

"Okay, Casey," Malinda said. "You're the experienced salvage master here. We'll do it your way and if we see that doesn't work, I'll call Ramon and see if he can do it."

"Good enough," Casey said, then looked at Luke. "Do ya think our bags will still inflate?"

"I don't see why not. They were in good shape the last time we used 'em."

"Okay, let's get 'em out. With the cables and the floats, I think we can get it to move. If it comes off the bottom enough, we'll move the boat, and *The Tide* should drift with it."

Casey and Luke busied themselves with getting the gear ready. I filled and cleaned the tanks while Jack cleaned the weapons. When the winch fires up and the cables get tension on them, the motor will make a lot of noise and draw attention to us. We'll probably get visitors.

Casey came out of the cabin pushing a dolly with a large box on it. "This is one of the airbags," he said as he dumped it on the fantail. "I've got two more. We're going to have to make sure the compressor is in good shape in order to inflate 'em."

"I'll check it out," Kailey said. She went to the old compressor and pulled the dipstick out to check the oil. I saw her checking the tension on the belt, so I went back to my tasks, knowing she would make sure the compressor was in good working order.

Walter was starting to get anxious. He trotted around the deck a few times, then barked.

"What is it, boy?" I asked.

He barked again. Then he moved to the rail and put his front paws on it, looking toward shore.

I followed his stare and saw an approaching boat. I didn't recognize this one, but the men did look familiar when they got closer. It was the men who were with Duran earlier.

They stopped short of my boat and called to me.

"What do you want?" I called back.

They drifted a little closer. "Duran wants you to know he has Rosalinda. You will do as he says, or she will meet with an unfortunate accident."

Malinda stepped to the rail. "Tell Duran I want to see him."

"And who might you be?"

"Brittany. Set up a meeting."

The two men in the boat changed their tune when they discovered who they were talking to.

"Yes, ma'am. We will make sure he gets the message."

"If Rosalinda is hurt, you will all pay," she said.

"Yes, ma'am," they repeated.

They turned their boat and sped away.

Kailey walked to Melinda's side. "You know if you go to meet with him, he'll kill you, don't you?"

"Yeah, I know. That's why you and Cam are going with me."

Kailey smiled. "My pleasure."

"We'll be ready tomorrow," Casey said. "We can hook up to *The Tide* in the morning."

"Good, everything should be set by then," I replied, my mind already wandering to the dangerous meeting we were about to have with Duran. I couldn't let him hurt Rosalinda, but I also couldn't let him hurt us.

As the night wore on, Kailey and I made sure we were well-armed and mentally prepared for whatever was to come. Walter stayed close to us, sensing the tension in the air.

Finally, one of Duran's men returned and told us the meeting was set for tomorrow morning on the beach near the marina.

We had a few drinks that evening and watched the sunset. We spoke a little about our meeting in the morning.

The next morning, we set out in the dinghy toward shore with Brittany at the helm. The sun was just beginning to rise, casting a warm glow across the water. But the beauty of the sunrise was quickly forgotten as we approached the shore and saw Duran and his men waiting for us.

Duran's eyes locked onto Brittany's, and he sneered. "I see you brought the whole gang with you. How sweet."

Malinda didn't flinch. "Where's Rosalinda?" she demanded.

Duran chuckled. "She's safe, for now. But I have a proposition for you. I'll give her back to you unharmed in exchange for your boat and all its contents."

Malinda's face hardened. "You want our boat? Over my dead body."

Duran's grin widened. "That can be arranged."

Suddenly, one of Duran's men raised his rifle. Kailey reacted like a snake striking. She threw her knife from her hip and hit the man in the throat.

He dropped his gun and held his throat as he gasped for air and went to his knees. Then he fell forward, dead.

No one said anything; they just looked at him. I took four steps to the right, and Kailey took four to the left. We all had our hands on our weapons.

"What now, Duran," Brittany asked. "You wanna make a move?"

Duran stood still, his eyes moving across the three of us. "I can have you arrested, you know," he said.

"Do it," Brittany said. "Don't forget to tell them who they're coming after."

"You have all the answers, don't you?" he said.

"Bring Rosalinda to me within the hour or we'll have a battle here."

Duran stood tall and puffed out his chest. "I'll bring her when I'm ready," he spat.

"That's fine, as long as it's within the hour. Where is Vinicio?"

"He resting. He'll be okay."

"If he's not, you're dead."

Duran swallowed hard.

Chapter 41

Duran had his men put the dead man in his jeep and left without saying another word. We sat at a little bar close to the marina and watched the tourists.

A half-hour later, Kailey announced she would go to another local bar nearby and watch us. "If I see any trouble, Duran will be the first to drop," she said.

Brittany nodded as Kailey stood and left.

"This might be dangerous, right?" I asked.

Brittany said, "Duran is, one, an asshole, two, a murderer, and three, proud. I might have insulted him too much in front of his men."

"Then I guess we had better be ready."

"It wouldn't hurt," she said, looking up and down the beach.

I took a sip from my drink. "I'm happy for you and Casey," I said. "I have always wanted you to be back with your family."

She looked at me sadly. "Yeah, me too. Too bad I have to leave and never see him again."

That surprised me. "What do you mean?"

"He'll be in too much danger. Duran knows we're together now. He'll tell others, and the word will spread."

I thought about that for a minute. It seems that the only way to stop Duran is to get something on him to keep him quiet.

"Does Casey know?"

"Not yet, but he knows we can't be seen in public together."

"We'll find a way to make it work."

I heard a vehicle coming toward us and looked up. Duran stopped his jeep in front of us and opened the door. Rosalinda stepped out.

"Here she is," he said, smiling. "I was never going to harm her. I have to go back to Cancun for a few days. I will be in contact with you when I return. I still want my share."

"Why do you think you have a share?" Brittany asked.

"Because I know who your friends are," he said and laughed. He got into his Jeep.

"You're right about one thing," I said. "He'll hold that over you."

Brittany stood and walked to the Jeep. "Where's Vinicio?"

The back door opened on the other side, then closed. The Jeep roared away. Vinicio was lying on the ground.

Brittany went to him. He rolled over and looked at her. "Sorry," he said.

"Are you okay?"

"Yeah, I'm fine," he said getting up slowly.

"Fuckin' prick. I think I might kill him."

"I need to make a call," Brittany said as Rosalinda came to us. "Excuse me."

Brittany walked away with her phone to her ear. Rosalinda sat next to me without saying a word.

"Are you okay?" I asked her. She nodded. "Did he hurt you?" She shook her head. "Can you come back to the boat with us?" she nodded again.

I let her be. She seemed to have had some kind of mental trauma. That is understandable. She probably had a good life here until Pedro came along.

Brittany returned and asked if we were ready.

"Yeah, Rosalinda is going to the boat with us."

"Good," Brittany said. "She'll be safer there."

Kailey showed up a minute later. "I watched until he disappeared down El Cuyo Road," she said. "What's going on?"

We told her about his conversation. "He's a dead man," Kailey said.

Brittany didn't comment. She just turned and headed for the marina. Something is up with her, and she doesn't want to share.

"I'll see you later," Vinicio said. "I have things to do. Rosalinda will be better with you."

"This wasn't your fault. Don't let it bother you.," I said. "Duran owns this area. That is until Brittany got here."

"Maybe it wasn't all my fault, but I still have a score to settle."

I couldn't stop him. I watched as he treaded down the road and disappeared into the town.

Back on *Malinda's Star*, we settled Rosalinda into a cabin and made her some tea. I couldn't help but feel sorry for her. She seemed so fragile and scared. I wished there was more we could do to help her.

As we sat in the galley, Brittany finally spoke up. "We need to talk about what happens next," she said, her voice serious.

"What do you mean?" I asked.

"I mean, we're running out of time. We'll be hoisting up the shipwreck tomorrow, and we still don't know what we're dealing with."

"With *The Tide*?" I asked.

Brittany shook her head. "With Duran."

"What about the police?" I asked. "Can't we go to them?"

Brittany scoffed. "And tell them what? That we're looking for a mythical treasure that may or may not exist, and Pascual Duran wants part of it. They'll think we're crazy."

"Why not, they know you."

"I would be too exposed. Right now, they probably think I was just here to protect my territory, but if I tell them I'm trying to find a treasure, they'll investigate."

"We need to get more information," Brittany said. "We need to find someone who knows about Duran. Someone who can help us figure out what we're dealing with."

"Who do you have in mind?" I asked.

Brittany looked at me, a glint in her eye. "Celio Zubia."

"Who's Celio?"

"Duran's lover."

"Do you know him?" I said, still trying to process the lover part.

"Yes, I do. But, if things go right, we won't have to worry about it anyway."

"Why's that?"

She shrugged the question off and asked Kailey if she had heard from Antonio.

"Yesterday," Kailey said. "Everything is set for next week."

That was the end of that conversation. I have learned not to ask questions of two assassins when they are discussing business.

"I think we're ready to go," Casey told me. "We'll get up early and start hooking the lines up. The girls can help you with that, and Luke is going to dive with me. We'll place the airbags inside and spread them out."

"Luke thinks he's strong enough?" I asked.

"He says he is. We'll see."

"Okay then, we'll go back to *The Same Old Song* and see you in the morning," I said, standing. "Get some rest."

Kailey, Malinda, Rosalinda, Jack, Walter, and I got into the tender and motored back to my boat a few hundred yards away.

We sat at the table on the upper deck, eating a cheese ball and having margaritas.

"I hope everything goes according to plan tomorrow," Jack said. "I have a bad feeling about this whole deal."

"I think we'll be okay. Casey has done this a few times over the years. He knows what he's doing," I assured him.

"Yeah, but the boat thing isn't what's getting me. It's all the trouble we've had with Pedro and Duran."

Malinda's phone rang. She stood and went inside. Kailey watched her nervously. Something was going on.

Brittany returned a few minutes later. She picked up her drink and downed it. I assumed everything didn't go as planned.

Kailey watched her, concerned. "Brit?"

"He got through," she said. "They think he went by boat."

"Who?" I asked.

"Duran. We had the road blocked. Somehow, he made it to Cancun."

"It's okay, Brit," Kailey said. "We'll get him when he returns."

"Meanwhile, we have a lot of work to do here," I said, trying to get her mind off Duran.

"I don't like that he got away from us," Malinda said.

"It's his land," Jack said. "He knows it better than we do."

"Yeah," she said then looked at me. "It's the perfect time to raise *The Tide*."

Malinda fixed her another drink and sat down. "It's already started," she whispered.

I asked her, "What has?"

"Casey. I'm too worried about him."

"Is Casey your boyfriend?" Rosalinda asked.

Malinda looked at her, "No, just a man who needs help."

That reminded us we had to be careful what we said in front of her.

We made small talk until I suggested we get some sleep. "It's a big day tomorrow."

That night in bed, Kailey and Malinda were quiet. We went to sleep as soon as our heads hit the pillow. Walter even passed out on the floor next to us.

My last thought before drifting off was, *Why did Duran give Rosalinda up so easily?*

Chapter 42

W e arrived at *Malinda's Star* at six a.m. Casey already had the crane over the water and the lines down.

He was folding the airbags so he could maneuver them easily once they were in the boat below.

Luke was lowering the winch on the crane. "We'll be ready in about fifteen minutes," he said.

"Sounds good," I said. "What do you want us to do?"

"Can you flip the outriggers into the water and lock them in place? They'll keep us from tipping over. When you're finished, suit up and join us in the water. We'll hook the lines to areas we talked about yesterday. We will probably have to make some adjustments, but we'll figure it out."

"Will do."

Jack and I released the pontoons and lowered them into the water. Once lined up, I slid the rod through the alignment holes and locked them in place.

The water was calm, and there was a slight breeze. I could feel the excitement and anticipation building inside me as I realized that this was it, the spot where *The Tide* lay at the bottom of the ocean.

Casey and Luke were already in the water, preparing to hook the lines up to the ship. Brittany and Kailey were standing on the deck, watching them intently. They had headphones so they could communicate with Casey. He will want them to tighten the line with the winch when he tells them to. Jack, Walter, and I were all on standby, ready to assist in any way we could.

We put on our wetsuits and tanks. The water was refreshing as we dove in to help hook the lines up.

As we got closer, I could see the dark silhouette of *The Tide* looming beneath the surface. It was a haunting and eerie sight, but also incredibly thrilling.

I could feel the power of the ocean all around me as I worked to guide the lines to the ship. It was a delicate operation, and one wrong move could send the whole thing tumbling back down to the ocean floor.

But Casey and Luke were professionals, and we worked together seamlessly to get the job done. After what felt like hours, we finally had all the lines hooked up and ready to go.

Casey signaled he was going inside to place and open the bags. Once they were opened, it would be time to connect the airlines. But we needed to be out of the way before any air was applied. The ship could move, crashing down on one of us or trapping us inside.

Luke and Jack fed the bags to Casey. I joined him inside and helped open them. The cavity seemed solid enough to hold the bags and lift the ship.

"Okay, let's do this," Casey said, signaling for us to surface.

When we were back aboard the ship, Casey told us to do whatever Luke said. Casey was going to go back down and watch the ship's reaction to the air being supplied to the bags. He would signal us when the air lines were attached.

"You be sure to watch from a safe distance," Luke said. "We don't want to turn this into a rescue mission."

"I'll be careful," he said.

Once the air lines were attached, Casey descended back into the water. I watched him go, feeling the weight of the task ahead of us settling on my shoulders. We were about to lift a shipwreck from the ocean floor, and anything could go wrong.

A couple of minutes later, Casey signaled he had the air lines hooked to the bags.

Luke began to slowly turn on the air, and I could feel the ship start to shift beneath our feet. It was a slow and steady process, but I could see the excitement building in Brittany and Kailey's eyes as they watched *The Tide* begin to ascend.

I took a deep breath and focused on my task. We had to make sure the lines stayed attached and the bags didn't burst. It was a delicate balance, and I could feel the sweat starting to bead on my forehead.

Suddenly, there was a loud pop, and the ship lurched to one side. I panicked for a moment, but then I saw Casey's signal from beneath the water. It was just one of the bags bursting, but we were still okay.

We worked quickly to adjust the lines and redistribute the weight.

• • • •

CASEY WATCHED AS THE airbag burst. A mountain of air bubbles rose to the surface. The ship that was just starting to move settled back to the ocean floor.

He swam closer to inspect the shifting from the collapse. Everything still looked okay, so he signaled to give it another try.

He saw the lines tighten and knew that Luke had ordered the lines taut. They were going to have to rely on them more now since they only had one bag.

The second airbag inflated to the point Casey thought it might rupture. He told Luke to stop the pressure and pull with the lines.

He watched as *The Tide* moved. It rocked port as the bow came off the ocean floor. A flume of air bubbles escaped from an unknown cavity deep within the ship.

Come on, baby. Keep moving. Soon, the bow was five feet off the bottom, and the stern started to lift. This is what they wanted. Soon Casey would signal Luke to stop and move *Malinda's Star* twenty yards starboard.

The Tide rose slowly but at a steady pace. Casey ordered them to hold where they were as he swam around the ship, inspecting the lines. They were all in place and holding steady.

"Up a little," Casey said. He watched as *The Tide* moved again. It was an eerie sight, watching a shipwreck rise. It was like the dead coming back to life.

He was surprised at the condition of the old warship. Its sleek lines were still visible beneath the barnacles. Where the hull had been submerged into the ocean floor, it almost looked as if it could sail again.

"She's off the floor," Casey said in Luke's ear. "Keep going. How's *Malinda's Star* reacting?"

Casey heard Luke's voice. "Steady as she goes," he said. "I don't think she even knows she's pulling a wreck off the bottom."

Casey smiled to himself behind his mask. This could be big. If we got this thing all the way to the surface, it might be worth a fortune in itself.

"Up," Casey said.

The ship rose. It was now twenty feet off the ocean floor. "Can you take it higher?" Casey asked.

"I can bring the damn thing to the surface, if you want," Luke said.

"That's what I wanted to hear. It's halfway there. Tie it on the outrigger side, and we'll see what we have."

As the ship rose slowly toward the surface, Casey swam closer to it, watching the lines. Then suddenly, the line on the bow slipped, and the ship shifted. It was coming toward Casey fast. He tried to get away from it, cursing himself for getting so close.

The Tide slammed into Casey, knocking his regulator out of his mouth as he felt a pain in his arm.

M*alinda's Star* shifted suddenly to port. It pulled the bow around about five feet, then jerked again. "I think a line slipped, but it's caught again!" Luke yelled. "Casey, can you hear me?"

Luke paused, waiting for Casey to tell him he was alright. "Casey!" he paused again. "Casey?"

"I'm going in," I said and dove over the side.

I took a deep breath before hitting the water and used the speed to take me down. I saw Casey drifting down and swam after him, kicking as fast as I could. His regulator was floating beside him, a steady stream of air flowing from it.

I caught him as I was about to run out of air. I took a hit of his air and shoved it into his mouth. Then I started a slow ascend. As I turned, I saw Malinda was right beside me.

As I passed *The Tide*, I looked at it for any sign it might release again. All the lines were taut. I kept a steady pace to the surface.

When we broke through, I gasped for air. My lungs were threatening to explode. I pulled Casey to the swim platform, where Kailey waited. She pulled him aboard and removed the regulator. Malinda began mouth-to-mouth, alternating with pumping his chest. Within thirty long seconds, he turned his head and spit water.

Malinda sat back on her ankles and let out a sigh of relief. Casey opened his eyes, looking around wildly. He tried to talk, but choked again. Turning his head, he threw up more water. Then he gasped, "Is *The Tide* okay?"

No one answered him. We were all amazed that he almost died and wanted to know if the bloody ship was okay.

"Well?" he asked, looking around.

"It looked fine to me," I said. "Can you sit up?"

He raised up and then grabbed his arm as he winced in pain. "Shit," he said. "I think I broke my arm."

Kailey inspected it. "I don't feel any bones. Can we cut your suit off?"

"Unzip it and try to get it off first," he said.

Kailey unzipped the suit and tried to slide it down his shoulders.

"Shit!" he yelled.

"Out of the way," Malinda said as she pulled a knife from her ankle. She held the suit out and cut it until it fell off Casey.

"Man, that was my best suit."

"You can buy a new one with all the money you're going to make," Malinda said.

Rosalinda watched from where she stood by the railing. She kept looking out to the horizon, watching.

"I'll suit up again and take his place," I said.

"Cam," Kailey said worriedly, and placed a hand on my shoulder. Then she removed it, knowing it wasn't going to do any good to tell me not to go. "Be careful."

When I was ready, I asked Luke if he was. He said any time but stay away from the ship. One down is enough.

I dropped into the water and swam close to *The Tide* but not so close that it could get me.

"I'm ready," I said into my mouthpiece. "Take it up slowly."

I watched as *The Tide* rose again. I could see why Casey was so excited about it. It was something no one would ever see again, this two-hundred-year-old warship coming to life.

I followed it from a distance, watching the lines as they strained under the weight. The remaining airbag was definitely doing its job. In spots, it was pushing through holes in the hull, but it looked as if it were holding.

I realized I was now only five feet from the surface. The cabin of *The Tide* and I broke through the surface together. I flipped off my mask and watched as it rose to fresh salt air and came to life back in the world it left behind two hundred years earlier.

I glanced at *Malinda's Star* and saw the railing was crowded. They were all staring in amazement at the once-in-a-lifetime spectacle.

After dropping below the surface for one last look. I climbed onto the platform and joined the others. It was a sight to behold.

"Did anyone film that?" I asked.

"We have it all," Luke said, pointing at a row of cameras on the wheelhouse. "How did your body cam work?"

"We'll have to see," I said, hoping I remembered to turn it on.

"Don't worry, Cam," Kailey said. "I turned it on when I hugged you."

That was a relief.

We pulled *The Tide* all the way to the surface, so the bow was sitting in the water as it had been so long ago. Water gushed from the holes in the fuselage, making the ship lighter. *Malinda's Star* responded to the loss of weight and straightened.

"We did it!" Casey yelled. "We got that fucker up."

"What now?" I asked.

"Now we take her to the beach, where we can explore every inch of her. Then we dive again and search the floor where she had laid for so long to see what she was hiding." Casey was talking so hard that he had to stop and take a deep breath.

"You can't dive," I said.

"Doctor Brittany said I was fine. Just bruised a bit."

I looked at Brittany. She shrugged.

Jack and I helped Luke secure *The Tide* to *Malinda's Star.*

"Will she pull the extra weight to the beach?" I asked.

"Shouldn't be a problem," Luke said.

Then Rosalinda spoke up. "Guys, I'm sorry. We have company," she said, pointing out to sea. "They said they would kill my family."

I turned to look in the direction she was pointing. Four boats were speeding toward us from the horizon. They would be here in four or five minutes.

"Who is it?" I asked her.

"Duran. I had to call him when *The Tide* surfaced. He said he would kill my family."

"Everyone get their weapons!" I yelled. "Jack and Kailey, come with me to *The Same Old Song*. We'll do better from two spots."

We jumped into the tender and sped to my boat. Once onboard, Walter ran into the salon. He has a knack for knowing when danger is afoot.

We checked our guns and kneeled along the gunwales. I looked at *Malinda's Star* and saw them doing the same. The four boats were almost to us now and coming fast.

I aimed my rifle at the first boat and tightened my grip on the stock.

As the first boat approached, I could see Duran at the helm, a smirk on his face. He was a ruthless man known for his violent tactics and disregard for human life. I knew we were in for a fight.

When I saw a mounted automatic on the bow of one of the boats start shooting at us, I knew it was time.

"Fire!" I shouted, and the sound of gunfire filled the air. I aimed carefully, trying to hit the engine of the first boat. The boat shook as my bullet hit its mark and it began to slow down.

But we were outnumbered, and the other three boats were still coming at us full speed. Bullets whizzed past my head, and I ducked down behind the gunwale.

"Cam, we can't take them all!" Kailey yelled.

I knew she was right. We had to come up with a plan and fast.

I saw the crew of *Malinda's Star* fire at the intruders as well. They spread out, realizing we weren't giving up without a fight.

Someone's bullet found its mark again, and the driver of the second boat fell over the side. Another man jumped in and took his place, but that left them with one less gunfighter.

I saw Duran's boat turn and head down shore. It didn't return. He had left his men there to fight as he retreated to safety.

Without their leader, they lost their strength and their willpower to be slaughtered. They were now sitting ducks for us, and they knew it. The two remaining boats turned to flee. One of them stopped next to the disabled boat and picked up their crew. Then they throttled down and left as fast as they could.

I realized the battle wasn't over when I saw the helicopter coming at us.

Chapter 44

"**G**et inside!" I yelled.

We barely made it inside when the sound of the helicopter whizzed over us, and the deck of my boat exploded into splinters. Those guys had some heavy shit on board. If we didn't stop them, we'd eventually sink.

I saw Malinda aiming at the helicopter with her sniper rifle. She squeezed off one shot, and the plane dove into the water. It pays to practice.

We returned to the deck to assess the damage. There was plenty of it, but nothing to keep us from going about our business.

I noticed something splashing in the water. "One of the helicopter crew survived," I said. "I'm going to go get him."

I took the tender out with Jack and pulled him in. He spoke in Spanish, but it was too fast to understand. I knew Malinda would get him to talk, so I motored to their boat.

"Is everyone okay?" I shouted.

"We're fine," Malinda said.

"Talk to this guy, will ya?"

Luke pulled the man onto his boat.

Malinda sat across from the captured man and stared at him intensely. Her eyes were cold and calculating, and the man squirmed under her gaze.

"Who do you work for?" she asked in a low voice.

The man hesitated for a moment before answering in broken English. "I work for Duran. He pay me to kill you."

Malinda leaned back in her chair, studying the man. "Why does Duran want me dead?"

The man shrugged. "I do not know. He just tell me to do it."

Malinda's eyes narrowed. "What else do you know?"

The man hesitated again before speaking. "There is something in the warehouse. Duran keep it there. He say it very valuable."

Malinda leaned forward, her interest piqued. "What is it?"

The man shrugged again. "I do not know. He keep it secret."

"Where is the warehouse?"

"Santa Maria, about a half hour."

"Yeah, I know where it is," she said. "Tie him up below," she told Luke.

She looked out toward shore and thought, *What could be so important that you would risk your life trying to kill me?*

Malinda turned and went to Rosalinda. "What else have you told him?"

"Nothing, I swear. He just told me to let him know when you had the treasure."

"We didn't have the treasure."

"I know. I didn't want him to have it."

"Do you know what's in the warehouse?"

"I overheard something about documents. But that's all I know."

Documents, Malinda thought.

"Did you hear the name Kolzak?" she asked, taking a long shot.

"No."

"What about Kiselev?"

She thought for a second, "Yes. I remember that name."

Malinda smiled and said, "Thanks."

"What's all that mean?" Luke asked.

"Kolzak Kiselev. He stole some top secret documents from the Kremlin. They have a formula that will allow them to hack into the missile bases in Russia. Even if they change the code, someone could still get in with these. It was built as a failsafe. If they fall into the wrong hands, we'll be fighting an invisible enemy."

"He sounds Russian. Won't he sell to them first?" I asked.

"They deny they were stolen. China has made a bid for the papers. He's not loyal to Russia. I just wonder how Duran got his dirty paws on them. Kolzak has vowed to use them first unless he is paid one hundred million dollars. He will destroy Australia first, then Hawaii, then The Bahamas until he gets paid."

"Why would Russia have such a code?"

"It's worse than it sounds," Malinda said. "That code will work for any missile base anywhere in the world."

"If they are as valuable as they seem to be, why would Duran worry about a measly treasure from this boat? And, why didn't he get them before Casey got here?"

"Sometimes enough just isn't enough. Maybe he's not the owner of the documents. He probably didn't know they were here until now."

We theorized what could happen if we didn't get the documents back. Malinda said she needed to make a call.

• • • •

"OLSEN, IT'S BRITTANY. I believe we have found the Kolzak documents."

"We need them, and soon. We're standing by at the Pentagon as we speak. We've received a message to turn on the screen in the war room. Wait," he said. Then Brittany could hear voices in the room. They were yelling, "No!"

Then there was a commotion as she heard an explosion.

"What happened?" she asked excitedly.

"He just blew up a passenger plane over Japan. Now there's a message coming across the screen."

Brittany waited while the message appeared. Then Olsen came back on. "Find him, Brittany. His message said this was an AI film. It didn't really happen this time, but next time it *will* happen at JFK."

"I'm on it. Send all available forces to Santa Maria, Yucatan. I'll do what I can until they arrive. I've got to go."

• • • •

WE HAD TO FIND OUT. And fast. We needed to get to Santa Maria, find the warehouse, and retrieve those documents before it was too late. But we couldn't just waltz in there and ask for them. We had to come up with a plan.

"Okay, here's what we're going to do," I said, looking around at everyone who had gathered on my boat. "We'll take the tender to shore and scout out the area. We'll find a way to get to the warehouse without being seen. Once we're there, we'll figure out how to gain access. When we have the documents, we'll get the hell out of there and destroy them."

Kailey nodded. "Sounds good on paper, but it won't be easy. We have to be careful. Duran's men will be everywhere along with Kolzak's crew."

"I know," I said. "That's why we need to move quickly and quietly. We don't want to attract attention."

"We need to blend in with the tourists," Brittany said. "We can take taxis."

"I have a truck," Rosalinda said. "We use it to get supplies for the café. There is room in the back for all of you to hide."

We looked at each other. It was hard to trust her again after getting burned the first time.

"It could work," Kailey said. "But we would have to tie her up in the back of the truck. We can't take the chance of her calling Duran again."

"That's okay," she said, "I'll do it."

"What about *The Tide*?" I asked.

"It's secure," Luke said. "We can leave it where it is for a day."

"You're not going with us," Malinda said. "You and Casey stay here and watch the boats. If you see anything, call us immediately. My team will be in El Cuyo shortly."

I went below and brought the prisoner topside, then put him in the tender with us. "We'll drop him off at the jail and deal with him later," I said.

We climbed into the tender and started the engine.

The sun was setting, casting an orange glow over the water. I couldn't help but feel a sense of foreboding. This was a dangerous mission, and we were in enemy territory.

As we approached the shore, we could see Mario waiting for us. He caught the lines and tied us off.

He greeted us cheerfully but soon picked up on the mood. When he saw us unload the bags with the guns in them, he asked if there was anything he could do to help us.

"Where is your father?" I asked him.

"He's at home. It's safe there now that Pedro is gone."

I told Brittany where Moctezuma was.

"Yes, it's on the way to Santa Maria," she said.

"I think Silvio might be valuable. He probably knows the warehouse. I'll call him."

Kailey went with Rosalinda to get her truck. Brittany called Vinicio and told him to meet the two girls there.

Brittany and I waited at the docks, going over a plan when a bullet ripped through the wooden post next to us. A second later, another shot came in, hitting our prisoner in the chest. He fell into the water and was gone.

Chapter 45

I lunged for the deck. Brittany was already submerged beneath the water, and Mario had vanished down the dock.

The air around me hissed as another bullet flew past, smacking against the dock only a few feet away. I crouched behind a metal cabinet, desperately trying to assess the source of the shots. A small building about forty yards away seemed to be the culprit. Squinting, I saw a single arm extending outward, holding an assault rifle. I fired off one shot blindly, but it missed its target.

At least he had stopped shooting. I called out for Brittany once more but still got no response. *Had she been hit with that first shot?*

Then I heard two quick shots from behind the building. As I watched, Brittany stepped out and walked toward me.

I stood and waited. All she said was, "I hope that truck gets here soon."

I was about to call Silvio when it arrived five minutes later with Vinicio driving. Rosalinda was next to him, and I assumed Kailey was in the back, under the canopy.

"Vinicio," I said, "I'm glad your back and okay."

"I'm fine, but Duran will be easier to handle now. A few of his men had horrible accidents." He smiled.

When I opened the back curtain, she was there with another man.

"Who's this?" I asked, watching the man cower and scoot toward the cab.

"Celio Zubia," Kailey said. "Duran's lover."

I climbed in. "Did you learn anything?"

"A little. I thought if he doesn't start talking, I'd let you kill him."

"Okay," I said, playing along.

"He's in the warehouse," Celio blurted out. "They have eight men with them."

I called Silvio as we made our way to Santa Maria. "Hello, Cam. Good to hear from you again."

"I'm afraid I'm calling for help."

"Anything," he said.

"We're almost to your location. Do you know a warehouse in Santa Maria?"

"Sure. There is only one."

"We have word that Duran and a Russian spy are there with stolen documents that could destroy the world. They have set up a communication base and are threatening to shoot down civilian aircraft's."

"That can't be, Cam. I was in Santa Maria yesterday. I drove past that warehouse. It is abandoned. The roof is even gone."

"Are you sure?"

"Si, señor. It is no more."

"Thanks, Silvio."

"Good luck, Cam."

I hung up and thought for a minute. "Stop the truck!" I yelled.

The truck stopped, and Brittany asked what the problem was.

"Silvio said the warehouse is abandoned and half gone. There is no way they could use it for a control center. I've been wondering why everyone is giving up information so easily. Now I know. He wants to create a diversion from the real location. The papers aren't in the warehouse, they're hidden on *The Tide*."

"Why would they do that?"

"It's a way to hide the documents and remain anonymous. He thinks no one will find them there, but then we came along. He sent Pedro to make sure that anything they found would be turned over to Duran. Then when Pedro died, Duran had to take over to get them. Kolzak Kiselev is pulling the strings. It's a way to conceal the evidence while still having immediate access to the documents. He was probably planning to sell them and give the location to the highest bidder. We screwed it up for them, and now they're trying to get us away from *The Tide*. If I'm right, we have to get back fast. They never were after the treasure. The real treasure is the documents."

I looked at Celio. He said, "I swear, he said at the warehouse."

"He knew we'd get Celio. They've been giving everyone the wrong information."

My cell rang. "Hello."

"Cam, we're under attack again," Casey said into the phone. "This time, we can't hold them."

"We're on our way. There's documents hidden in *The Tide*. That's what they want."

We spun the truck around and drove toward El Cuyo. There was no way we were going to make it before the attackers overpowered Casey and Luke.

Brittany was on her cell shouting out orders to her team. They were in El Cuyo now and had access to a boat. "Call Key West Naval Base," she shouted. "Find a carrier."

I knew she was calling in fighter jets. This was going to be explosive.

• • • •

CASEY STOOD AT THE gunwale, firing his rifle. He looked at Luke, who was reloading his. Luke looked up. "We're almost out of ammo."

Casey looked back at the six boats that were now moving closer. "Make every shot count," he said.

Casey fired again and watched a man drop into the boat. It did nothing to deter the aggressors.

Then Casey heard two more boats coming from El Cuyo. "It looks like they have backup!" He yelled to Luke.

But the boats passed them and went straight for the boats that were attacking them. The men in the two boats opened fire on the others but were definitely outgunned. Casey opened fire on them again, too, hoping that together they could overpower them.

The boats split up and surrounded Casey's boat. Even with the help, they were losing the battle.

. . . .

WE ARRIVED AT EL CUYO and could hear the gunfire on the horizon. A crowd of tourists and curious locals were standing on the beach watching the water. They could see the boat's lights and hear the gunfire, but had no idea how serious it was.

The moon was shining now, and we were taking a chance going out there with lights on, but we had no choice.

The only boat we had was the tender we came in, and we would be sitting ducks in it. I scanned the marina for a better one.

Mario ran to us. He pointed to *Malinda's Star* and yelled, "Mister Casey is in trouble!"

"I know. Do you have a bigger boat we can use to go help him?"

Mario looked at the marina. He pointed to a thirty-foot Chris Craft. "I'll get the key," he said and ran back to his hut. We picked up our bags and ran to the boat.

He met us there as we threw our guns inside. He tossed me the keys and untied the lines. We left Rosalinda on the dock and headed toward the commotion.

Halfway to the boat, Brittany's phone rang. She listened and hung up. She called her crew. "Get Casey and Luke and get out of there." She listened again and hung up.

I was speeding toward *Malinda's Star* when Brittany told me to stop. I looked at her like she was crazy.

"Just stop. Trust me," she said. I did.

We watched her crew slide beside *Malinda's Star* and saw Luke and Casey jump in. The boat spun away and came toward us. When it reached us, they cut their engines and sat beside us.

"They're going to board the boat and get the documents," Casey said.

Brittany cocked her head and listened. "No, they're not."

Then I heard it, too. Jets. I could see two of them flying just off the water, heading straight at the boats. Gunfire erupted, and the boats exploded one at a time.

The jets circled and made another pass, finishing the boats off. Then they disappeared back over the horizon where they had come from.

We watched from our position 300 yards away. "Jesus, did that really just happen?" Casey asked, looking at Brittany.

"It happened," she said. "And we're going to have some explaining to do."

A few minutes later, as we were climbing aboard *Malinda's Star*, police and coast guard boats began to appear.

Brittany stood alone on the platform and motioned them to the boat. She was talking, and I could see their captain writing something down in a notebook. He dipped his head and gave her a slight salute.

The police checked each boat, looking for survivors, but there were none.

They had the waters cleared and gone in under two hours.

"What now?" Luke asked.

"Now we search *The Tide* for those documents," I said. We'll get her to shore and beach her so she'll be more stable. First thing in the morning."

We accessed the damage to Casey's boat and checked the riggings holding *The Tide* "We'll be okay for tonight," I said.

We sat at the table on the fantail and discussed the day. "Did anyone see Duran in any of the boats?" I asked.

No one had. That meant he was still out there somewhere, and he probably wasn't going to give up.

We finished our drinks and decided to turn in for the night. Casey said he would take the first watch, and I would relieve him in three hours. Jack said he would relieve me two hours after that.

The next morning, Casey fired the large engines up and throttled toward the beach about a half-mile from town. When we felt *The Tide* hit bottom, we anchored *Malinda's Star* and climbed aboard *The Tide*.

The first thing Jack did was to go to the hatch he had pried open. "I think there might be something hidden in here," He said. "It was too easy to open after two hundred years."

"Yeah, I agree with ya," I said. "Let's have a look."

We pried the hatch open again and showed a light inside. I noticed a wire attached to the hatch lid. I pulled the wire, and eventually, a waterproof box appeared. I twisted the wire off of it and turned to Brittany. I extended the box and said, "I don't want to know what's inside."

She took the box and disappeared into the cabin with Kailey. They reappeared a couple of minutes later. "We have it," she announced. "I need to leave."

"That's great news," I said. "I'll take you back to El Cuyo."

"That's okay. My ride will be here in a few minutes."

"Hey, guys!" Casey yelled, "Come here a minute!" he seemed excited about something. "Look in here," he said, pointing to the hatch we had found the documents in.

We turned the light in again and took turns looking into the small opening. Gold. Shining like it was in a jewelry store. A large pile of shiny trinkets and some gold bars.

"There's more here than was in the other chest," Casey said. "Between the two, there's millions."

Chapter 46

Forty-five minutes later, a seaplane landed nearby and taxied to us.

"There's my ride," Brittany said.

I hugged her and then let her and Casey have some time together. After they talked, I expected to see Casey sad, but he actually looked excited.

She got on the plane, waved to us, and they took off. I was sorry to see her go, but I was glad she was taking the documents to the Pentagon.

"Okay, " I said, "I think we need to find something we can reach down inside the hole with and pull out the treasure a little at a time."

While we were searching the boat for just the right tool, I heard a boat approach. I looked up to see Mario bringing my tender out to us. He threw me the line, and I tied him off. He climbed onboard.

"That was the wildest thing I've seen in my whole twelve years," he said. "You guys really showed them."

"Yeah, I guess we did," I said. "Thanks for bringing my boat out."

"No problem. I wanted to get the other boat and tell you I saw Duran and Rosalinda leaving the beach area together a while ago."

"Together?"

"*Si*, but she didn't look too happy. I don't think she wanted to go. They watched the action out here, and then he took her arm and pulled her away."

Casey who didn't hear the conversation, spoke up from across the deck. "Hey Mario, come here a second."

Mario went to the other side of the deck.

"Step over this railing, but be careful. This old ship is full of holes," Casey said.

Mario stepped over as Casey led him to the hatch.

"Do you think you can fit through that hole?" Casey asked.

Mario looked at the hole and then up at Casey. "No problem," he said. "Why?"

"There's a treasure in there, and we need someone who can hand it out to us."

"How much do I get for such a dangerous job that no one else can do?" Mario asked, suddenly sounding grown up.

Casey scratched his chin, pretending to be thinking. "How about twenty dollars?"

Mario scratched his chin, "Hum, I was thinking like around ten thousand dollars."

"Hum," Casey said. "How about one percent?"

"How much treasure is in there?"

"Probably around three million."

"Thirty thousand?" Mario said quickly. He stuck his hand out to shake Casey's. "Deal."

Mario kicked off his sandals and climbed up to the hatch. He stuck his legs inside and slid in.

"Here ya go," Casey said, handing him a flashlight.

Mario took it and turned it on. We all gathered around the hatch, waiting for the first piece of gold.

"There's nothing here," Mario said, sticking his head back through the hatch.

"What? That can't be," Casey said.

Mario laughed and pulled his hand up. In it, he was holding a big wad of gold chains.

Casey took them, and Mario disappeared again. He kept sticking his hands through the hatch with more gold. We took turns taking it from him and finally made a line to *Malinda's Star,* where we could hand it over and stack it on the deck. Walter kept running from one end of the line to the other, watching every move as if he knew what was happening.

When Mario got to the gold bars, he could only lift one at a time through the hole. There were thirty-two in all.

After what seemed an eternity, Mario popped up and said, "That's all."

"Okay," Casey said, smiling from ear to ear. "That was a lot more than I thought would be in there."

"If I can help you find more treasure, could I get two percent?" Mario asked.

"Sure, if you can find any."

"Good, there's another hatch."

"What other hatch?" Casey asked.

"In here. I might be able to open it. Give me a crowbar."

Casey handed a crowbar through to Mario, who then started to pry another hatch we didn't know was there. We could hear Mario grunting while pushing on the bar. Then we heard a big crash and the crowbar clanging against the deck.

"Are you okay?" Casey yelled in.

There was no answer. "Mario!" still no answer. "Mario!" Casey yelled again.

Then Mario popped his head through the hatch again. "Do I get two percent of this treasure?" he asked.

"There's more?"

"*Si*, a little," Mario said, acting uninterested.

"Yeah, sure," Casey said.

Mario smiled and said, "I'll be right back."

The gold and silver he handed through this time had to outweigh the first load by fifty pounds.

When we were all finished, the pile of gold and silver lying on *Malinda's Star* deck looked like a mountain. There was probably fifty million dollars worth lying there.

"And you have the other duffel bag, too," I reminded.

Casey sat down on the deck and just stared at the treasure. "We're all going to be rich," he said.

"I don't need any," I said, "but I think Jack deserves some."

"Jack will be taken care of. I promise," Casey said, looking at Jack.

"Wow," Jack said.

Luke finally spoke up, "I knew we could do it," he said. "I knew if we kept at it year after year, one day it would pay off."

Kailey said, "You guys deserve this. You worked hard for it and almost lost everything."

Casey smiled with gratitude. "We couldn't have survived this without you guys. I can't wait to show Rosalinda."

I glanced at Mario who met my eyes, his expression grave. "Duran has her, mister Casey," he said, his voice quiet.

The smile dropped from Casey's face, and his brow furrowed in confusion. "Has her? What do you mean?"

Mario explained how Duran had taken Rosalinda away when they had left her on the beach a while ago. Anger and determination lit up Casey's features, and he turned to survey the beach of El Cuyo, his jaw set. "I have to go get her," he said resolutely.

Jack stepped up. "I'll go with you," he offered.

Casey shook his head. "Someone has to stay here and watch the treasure."

"Luke can do that," Jack suggested, and I nodded in agreement. "I'm going with you too," I said, my heart beating faster at the prospect of another adventure. Kailey chimed in after me, ready for an adventure as well.

"Walter and Luke can watch the boat," I said. "I suggest we get this treasure inside and hidden somewhere. There will be some curious tourists and locals coming this way to see *The Tide*."

"Let's get to work," Casey said.

Ten minutes later, part of the treasure was secured in a safe in Casey's room, and the other part in a closet in Luke's room.

"Let's go," Casey said, heading toward the tender.

"Thanks, Mario," I said sincerely. "Don't say a word about the treasure to anyone. If you do, you might lose your future."

Mario slid his finger across his lips as if he were zipping them closed.

"Good. Get in the tender, and we'll drop you off at the other boat."

We took Mario to the boat and waited while he started it. "Remember," I said and slid my finger across my lips as we pulled away from him.

El Cuyo isn't a large town, but it seemed that way when we stepped off the dock and looked at it.

"Which way?" Casey asked.

"We're going to have to split up," Kailey said. "Everyone keep your cell phones handy."

We decided who would take what route. We'd meet at the other end of town. El Cuyo had its share of tourists today. A large group was still standing on the beach talking about the jets that blew the boats up earlier. One boy was taking pictures of the tourists as they posed on the beach with the now-empty gulf behind them. He had made a sign the tourists held up saying 'War of El Cuyo 2023.' His tip jar was filling up.

I took the south side of the town, working my way east. I stepped into every restaurant and bar I passed, asking the locals if they had seen Duran or Rosalinda. They all knew who both of them were, but no one had seen them.

As I was talking to the owner of a small beer stand along the street, my cell phone rang. It was Jack.

"Cam, Duran is in Restaurant El Camaron. It's at the southeast end."

"I'm almost there," I said.

"That's not all. He's holding Kailey at gunpoint."

I arrived two minutes later and saw Jack and Casey standing outside the restaurant. It was empty other than Duran and Kailey.

"She walked in to check it out, and he was in there with a gun," Jack said. "I saw Rosalinda run out the back when he pointed the gun at Kailey."

"So, he's traded Rosalinda for Kailey now, thinking it will give him more leverage," I said.

I walked toward the café, watching his every move.

"That's close enough, Cam," he said. "I don't want to kill anyone, but I will. All I want is some of the treasure you found out there and one piece in particular that won't be of any use to you. It seems my career as a politician is ruined now because of you."

"If you mean the documents, they're on their way to the Pentagon."

I saw his shoulders slump. "Then I will need more of the treasure," he spat.

"What have you done with Kolzak Kiselev?" I asked him, trying to take his mind off Kailey long enough for her to do her thing.

"He had an accident. Most unfortunate. If he would have told me earlier that the documents were on *The Tide,* we wouldn't have all this mess. But I just found out yesterday. I really was just after some of the treasure to begin with. I was going to find a way to get the documents, but then I found out they were all connected. Now, all I have is the treasure and I want half of it or I will kill this beautiful woman."

"You know we're not going to give you any of the treasure, don't you?"

"Then I guess I'll just kill this little lady and then get Rosalinda and use her. I will give you only five seconds to change your mind."

He held the gun to her head and started to count the seconds off. When he got to three, his eyes opened widely, and he staggered back. He turned to look at Rosalinda, who was standing at the doorway of the café. I could see the knife sticking out between his shoulder blades. He raised the gun toward her just as Kailey hit him hard on the neck. He crumpled to the ground.

I went to him to see if he was still alive. He was, but just barely.

Casey ran to Rosalinda, who was still standing in the doorway staring at the man on the ground.

Casey hugged her. "Are you okay?"

She fainted, and he caught her, picking her up and carrying her inside.

"You okay, Kailey?" I asked.

"Yeah, fine. What about him?" she asked, looking down at Duran.

"He's breathing."

"Shit, I'm losing it," Kailey said, then bent down and held her hand over his nose and mouth. She stood back up and said, "He didn't make it."

The police, accompanied by a medical staff, came and took Duran away. The captain asked me how much longer I was going to be in town.

"I'm leaving as soon as possible," I said. "I've had all the vacation I can handle."

• • • •

THAT EVENING, SITTING on *Malinda's Star*, we talked about all the things we could do with the money. Jack has never had a million dollars. He said he would help some of the people down at the dock where he had his charter boat.

Kailey told them not to give her anything. Her reward was getting the documents safely back into the hands of the Pentagon. Besides, I knew she had over four hundred million already.

Mario, who had Walter in his lap, wanted to know how long it would be before he got his money.

"Oh, it usually takes about fifteen years to get things like this settled," Casey said.

"Ten percent, compounded daily," Mario said.

"Damn, boy, you need to open a bank," Casey said. "I'll have it to you in about a week."

Rosalinda punched Casey on the arm, "Why do you give that sweet boy so much grief?"

"Sweet boy?" Casey said, looking around the boat. "Where?"

I asked Casey when he would be going to The Bahamas.

"Not until I'm called," he answered. "But I'm happy. I know the time will come."

We didn't say any more about that. We can't let anyone know Brittany is Casey's sister.

"What will you do with your share?" Casey asked Mario.

"I am going to buy a new bicycle for me and one for Tito, and a boat for my father. Then I will buy us a new house with a doghouse in the backyard for my new Golden Retriever."

"Very good," Casey said.

"And some ice cream," Mario added.

We laughed. It was a pleasant evening sitting on *Malinda's Star* with the shadow of *The Tide* looking down on us. This great ship sat on the ocean floor for two centuries before we came along and brought it back into our world. The world it had come from. Though the ship itself was quite valuable, Casey decided to donate it to the Maritime Museum in Yucatan.

He would tow it to their docks, where a crane would place it outside on display.

"What will you do now, Rosalinda?" I asked.

She smiled at Casey. "She's going with me," he said, kissing her.

I was pleased with that. I excused myself and made a phone call.

"Did I wake you?" I asked.

Diane answered in a sleepy voice, "No, is everything okay there?"

"Couldn't be better. I've got a deal for ya."

When I returned to the others, they were standing next to *The Tide*, shining their flashlights around the hull.

"It came from over here," Casey was saying.

"What's up?" I asked.

"Someone called to us from here," Jack said. "We all heard it."

"What did they say?"

"Help me," Casey said.

"Is someone in there?"

"We haven't seen anyone. Do you believe in spirits?" Casey asked me as we stepped closer to the boat.

I felt a chill run through my body. Casey shined the light into the hatch we had pulled the treasure from. Then he jumped back.

"Shit," he said. "Look."

He handed me the light. I didn't know if I wanted to look. I leaned over cautiously and pointed the light inside. That's when I felt something grab my leg and cry out. I jumped and screamed. I turned to look down at my leg and saw Mario squatting there. Everyone started laughing.

When I caught my breath, I said, "You guys are really funny. I think I just lost ten years of my life."

"You sounded like a little girl," Jack said.

"Remember, payback," I told them.

As the evening wore on, we told stories of all that had happened while we looked for the treasure. I knew these stories would be told over and over again. Sometimes they would be told over a few beers in a pub somewhere in the Caribbean, and the stories would grow in intensity, including my reaction to the spirit.

I stood an hour later and said I thought it was time to head back to *The Same Old Song*. Kailey and Jack stood too.

"What's the plan for tomorrow?" Jack asked.

"Well, I thought we'd go ashore and try to enjoy the town for a change. It seems to be bustling with tourists, and I expect there will be more showing up to see *The Tide*.

"That sounds good, but I wish Diane were here now since all the trouble is over."

"You can bring her back in a week or so after you get all that money."

"I think I will," he said thoughtfully.

"Mario, do you want me to take you to the dock?" I asked him.

"No, I think I will sleep right here on the deck tonight. I can look at the stars."

"Okay, then. I hope the spirits don't get you."

He laughed nervously.

Kailey, Jack, Walter, and I stepped into the tender. Then I felt it move. I turned to see Mario climbing in. "I think I will sleep on your boat tonight," he said.

We set off across the water to *The Same Old Song*.

Chapter 48

We slept soundly for the first time in a week. It was almost eight o'clock before I felt Kailey untangle her naked body from mine.

I got up and pulled my shorts on. The coffee was already going as I entered the galley. Mario was standing in the doorway, looking out.

"What ya looking at?" I asked.

He jumped and spun around. "I didn't hear you," he said.

I walked to the door and looked out. Walter was sleeping on the deck with all four legs straight up in the air.

"That is a strange dog," Mario said.

"Sometimes, it gets worse," I said and poured myself a cup of coffee.

"Did you sleep good?"

"I did. How about you?"

"Okay, I guess," he said. Then he turned toward me and asked, "Do you think there are such things as spirits?"

So that's why he didn't sleep well. I had scared him. Now I felt bad.

"I do think there are some out there," I said. "But I believe they are good. They watch over and protect you. Have you heard of guardian angels?"

"*Si.*"

"Those are good spirits. If you're a good person, you'll have one watching over you. If you're a bad person, then you might attract the wrong kind of spirit."

He looked to be giving this some thought. I figured he was evaluating himself. He smiled, "I'll have good spirits watching over me," he said, then turned to watch Walter.

I opened the door and stepped onto the deck. "Walter," I whispered. I didn't want to scare him.

He opened his eyes and fell over sideways. Then he closed his eyes and went back to sleep.

Jack appeared next, then Kailey. It was a beautiful morning. We didn't have a big breakfast, instead, we had coffee and Pop-Tarts. Mario seemed to like them. "I had one of these one time," he said. "It was strawberry, but I think I like this chocolate better."

A small skiff motored up to our boat. Silvio was at the wheel. "Mario!" he called.

Mario waved from the deck. I asked Silvio if he wanted some coffee.

"No, thank you. We have some work to do. I hope to see you again."

Mario shook our hands and said he would see us at the dock when we come to town. I watched them slide through the water back to their world.

I knew Mario's money would give them a better life. That alone would give me a better life. Casey had told me that he was going to give Mario and Tito one million dollars each. Since Tito didn't have any family, Casey would set up a trust fund for him. He will be taken care of for life.

Kailey slipped her arms around me from behind. "Do you ever wish you had a son?" she asked.

I turned to face her. "With you?"

She smiled. "Maybe."

"I could live with that," I said. "If he was like Mario or Tito."

Then I heard a plane approaching. I had Jack and Kailey join me at the gunwale. I pointed to a seaplane that was about to sit down in the water. It splashed down and taxied to our boat.

"Who's that?" Jack asked.

"I ordered some chocolate honey buns from Key West."

We met the boat at the swim platform. The pilot got out and threw me the line, which I tied off.

Then the back door opened, and Diane and Stacy got out.

"Son of a gun," Jack said, pulling Diane to him.

I pulled Stacy onboard and hugged her.

"You're forgiven," she said.

I got the bags while Kailey talked with the two girls. She was already telling them what they were going to do today. They were all quite excited. Walter was running in circles. Now he had all his favorite girls with him, as did I. He knew there would be plenty of scratching and loving––as did I.

I asked Pete if he wanted to stay for the day. "No can do, Cam. I have more charters waiting."

We talked for a while and had coffee. Diane pulled a box of donuts out of her bag, and we all indulged.

After the coffee and donuts, Pete pushed off, saying he would see us back in Key West.

"I wanna see this boat you guys pulled up," Stacy said.

"It's right over there," I said, pointing to *Malinda's Star*.

Stacy read the name on the side of the ship. "*Malinda's Star*?" then she looked at me in puzzlement.

"Don't ask," I said.

She looked back at the ship. "Wow, is that it next to ...?"

"Yep, that's it, and it was jampacked with gold."

"Wow," she said again.

Diane slipped her arm around me. I did the same. "Kailey's been telling me a little about what you guys have been through. I told you it was a bad idea for you to go anywhere alone."

"It wasn't my fault."

"Maybe not this time, but you found trouble anyway."

"Your boyfriend is rich now."

"So I heard. I do thank you for that."

"Do you girls want to see *The Tide*?"

"Let us change, and we'll be ready," Stacy said.

They disappeared into the cabin as we finished our coffee. Jack put his hand on my shoulder. "Thanks for bringing them here," he said.

"My pleasure."

When the girls returned, I knew it was going to be another day of conflict in town. Their suits barely covered them. The men in town would be watching.

"Shall we?" Diane said.

"Sure, why not?" I answered, relenting.

We took the tender to *Malinda's Star* and climbed aboard.

Casey and Luke waited for us at the platform. When Casey saw Diane, he hugged her. "Wow, it's been a long time."

"Too long, Casey. Let's not wait so long again."

They broke their embrace as Luke stepped forward. Casey introduced Luke and Rosalinda to Diane and Stacy. Luke couldn't take his eyes off Stacy. She held his stare as well. When it finally became awkward, I said, "They want to see *The Tide*."

"Oh, yeah," Luke said, taking Stacy's hand. "Right this way."

He led her to the old warship and explained everything to her. "Right there's where we found the treasure."

"Why did you bring the ship up?" she asked.

"So we could get in the hidden hatch."

"How did you fit in there?"

"We have a secret weapon. You'll meet him in a while."

"Was there more treasure under the ship when you pulled it up?"

We all looked at each other. We had forgotten that was the reason we were going to move the ship in the first place.

"I don't know," Luke said. "We forgot to look."

I thought about it for a minute, then asked, "Do you girls want to dive?"

They were all excited about the prospect of finding gold. I had taught Stacy how to dive about six months ago. Diane was an old hand to diving.

Luke got all the equipment and handed it out. He fitted Stacy's to her body, very slowly. We took the tender back to *The Same Old Song* to get our gear.

"We'll take this boat out," I said. "If we find any treasure, it wouldn't fit in the tender with all of us."

We motored back to the spot where *The Tide* had rested for two centuries. I wasn't sure what we'd find down there. I didn't look at the area once the ship was lifted.

We dropped into the crystal blue water one at a time. We were four couples now enjoying a dive. The visibility was unlimited.

As soon as we arrived at the old graveyard, Stacy reached down and picked up a coin. It was covered in barnacles, but there was no doubt it was a gold coin.

We slowly covered the area, splitting up into twosomes. Soon, we realized we were going to need something to hold the coins.

I signaled to them and swam to the surface. I got three large net bags and dropped them back into the water.

I handed them out, and it didn't take long to fill them to the point that we wouldn't be able to get them to the surface if we didn't stop.

We took them up and went back down. When we came up the next time, we were satisfied we had exhausted the hunt.

We emptied the last bag and stood back, looking at the find. More millions, no doubt.

"Jeez, Casey," Diane said. "You guys are going to be filthy rich now."

"We already are," he said, looking at Luke. Luke nodded his head. "This is for all of us."

We celebrated hard that day. The girls danced in the bars to the island music while we told stories of our battles. The stories were already growing.

Luke asked if Stacy had a boyfriend. "Sometimes," I said. "You never know."

But I could tell by the way she was looking at Luke while she spun around the floor she just might be available.

There was one thing I knew for sure, even though Walter is good company, the cruise home will be a lot more fun than the cruise here.

The following morning, while we sat on the deck taking in the salt air, I realized that Stacy wasn't among us.

"Where's Stacy?" I asked them.

"Luke came over late last night and picked her up. She's on *Malinda's Star*," Diane said.

"Interesting."

"We estimated that yesterday we all ended up with about five-hundred-thousand. I think Stacy might have the fever now."

"I hope I didn't do the wrong thing by bringing her here," I said thoughtfully, looking toward *Malinda's Star* in the distance.

"I think she'll be fine," Diane said. "She's a strong girl."

I broke off a small piece of my roll and held it down for Walter. I waited before looking down and realizing Walter wasn't there.

"Where's Walter?"

"He went with Stacy," Kailey said.

"He's definitely a hound. He's going to be pissed when he finds out that we had more rolls."

"Are you girls ready to spend a day on the beach with some good food and rum?" I asked.

"Can't wait," Diane said.

"I'm in."

I heard the sound of the tender coming toward us. It was Luke, Casey, Stacy, and Rosalinda, with Walter leading the way from the bow.

"Ahoy!" Casey shouted.

We assisted them in getting on board.

"It's a beautiful morning," Stacy said. She looked invigorated.

"Yes, it is," I said. "Did you have a good night?"

She smiled at me and turned red. "Yep."

Luke spoke up. "I wanted to ask you if it is okay if Stacy stayed out here with me for a while."

"Why are you asking me?"

"She says you're her guardian. She won't do anything without your approval."

I looked at Stacy. "Please. Rosalinda's going," she said.

I didn't consider her my ward, but now that they asked...

"What about Hank?" I asked her.

"Barbie is there. She can watch him until I get back."

"What are you going to be doing?" I asked.

"We're going to stop and check out the *Santa Rosalie*." Luke said.

"Another treasure boat?"

"It's rumored to have millions onboard."

"She'll be okay, Cam," Casey said.

"What about pirates?"

"We have plenty of protection, and I'll call Brittany and have her send more. Now that I have money, I can do that."

"What if she gets homesick?"

"I'll call Pete. He'll come and pick her up."

I thought it over for a minute. They seemed to have an answer for everything. I said, "If it's what you want, then go for it."

Stacy hugged me. I felt like a father of two now. Diane and Stacy were grown women, but I realized they wouldn't do anything I didn't want them to do.

Kailey slipped her arm around me and whispered, "You're going to make a wonderful father."

· · · ·

THREE DAYS LATER, WE pulled the anchor up and set our course toward Key West. This wasn't the relaxing vacation I had hoped for, but it was a very satisfying escape.

Even though it was dangerous, I was able to spend time with all of my favorite people. Stacy might have found the love of her life. But I expected it wouldn't be too long before she returned to Key West.

I couldn't get Kailey off my mind. She's never talked about having kids before. She's the right age for it, but her life wouldn't allow for her to be a parent.

As I watched the sun rising on the horizon, I couldn't help but think how lucky I was. Still staring at the soft yellow and orange glow of the sun on the water, I reached for the table to pick up my roll. I felt around a bit for it before I looked at the table. My roll was gone.

"Walter!"

The End

Sign up for my NEWSLETTER[1] and receive the latest on my releases and other Tropical News. Plus, you'll receive the Free Prequel to the series. www.macofortner.com

. . . .

About Mac Fortner

MAC FORTNER IS A TROPICAL Adventure Author who was born in Evansville, Indiana but was never one to hang around one area too long. He lived for eighteen months in the Philippine islands and a year in Saigon. When he returned to Evansville, he spent time on his boats on the Ohio River.

This only fed his thirst for adventure, and he now lives in Florida three months out of the year with his wife, Cindy. They love spending time traveling the Florida Keys, where his protagonist, Cam Derringer, finds trouble around every turn.

He has been a full-time author since 2013 and now writes overlooking the beach and the Gulf of Mexico, but longs for the time when he can call Key West home.

You can join Mac's newsletter at www.macofortner.com and get your free prequel to the series. There you will be informed when a new book or new deal is coming out.

. . . .

THE NEXT BOOK, LOST Souls Of Key West, is in the works.

---

1.   https://dl.bookfunnel.com/z1rpfqxulr

www.ingramcontent.com/pod-product-compliance
Lightning Source LLC
Chambersburg PA
CBHW021429150726
47989CB00001B/180